BROI

By the same author:

Broken Cross

ROB FROST

MONARCH PUBLICATIONS
Tunbridge Wells

First published 1992

ISBN 1 85424 190 7

Front cover design by Vic Mitchell

British Library Cataloguing in Publication Data
A catalogue record for this book is available from
the British Library.

Production and Printing in England
for MONARCH PUBLICATIONS
Owl Lodge, Langton Road, Speldhurst, Kent TN3 0NP by
Nuprint Ltd, Station Road, Harpenden, Herts AL5 4SE.

Acknowledgements

This book would not have appeared without the help of Stephen Deal, who rescued me from an impossible deadline and who worked so hard on the revision of the second draft.

Thanks also to Marian Arthur and Karen Williams who toured the country planning and preparing the *Gospel End* tour, and whose support in this mad enterprise was invaluable. We're also indebted to the thousands of people in the national production team who have worked so hard to make this project work.

A special mention to Richard and Meryl Smith, Michael Whelton, and my wife Jacqui, who ploughed through endless pages of typescript making helpful suggestions. Tony Collins, my publisher, gave consistent encouragement, and Colin Reeves, editor of Christian Herald, gave us the title.

To the Seed Teams, and those willing to live on the front-line of mission in places like Redbrook.

Chapter One

The red removal van edged its way up the main road leading to Redbrook. It's wipers scraped back and forth smearing the drizzle over the windscreen. There was a long stream of traffic ahead, progress was very slow, and vehicles were barely moving at all. The driver silently cursed the numerous cars parked on double yellow lines which forced him to move into the path of the slow on-coming traffic. He negotiated the van round an obstructing white Vauxhall and crept forward another fifteen yards.

Somewhere behind him the driver could hear an ambulance siren. 'What chance do they stand, with this kind of traffic,' he muttered, bumping the removal van onto the pavement in the hope that the ambulance might squeeze by.

Gradually the ambulance edged past, its siren wailing and its lights flashing with frantic urgency. The attendant waved his arm in gratitude, and slowly the ambulance made its perilous way up the centre of the road.

Some minutes later the removal van passed the scene of a road traffic accident. A small black boy was being lifted into the back of the ambulance on a stretcher, his mangled bicycle lying bent and broken on the zebra crossing. Nearby a man stood next to a police car, blowing into a plastic bag. Stupid fool, thought the driver. London life.

Eventually the van drew into a busy London terrace and waited for a young man to remove some planks and dustbins that had obviously been placed there to reserve a space. It took a full five minutes of careful manoeuvring to edge the long vehicle into the parking space. With a grateful shudder the engine died.

'Wake up, we're here.' His two colleagues opened bleary eyes and gazed out at the squat little houses, the constant flow of traffic, and looming overhead the rows of tall tower blocks which overshadowed the older terraced houses. Somewhere in the distance they heard a police siren wailing.

'Blimey. What a dump,' one of them muttered.

The young man, who had removed the various planks and dustbins, greeted them warmly as they descended, yawning and stiff, from the cab.

'Good journey?' he inquired as he shook hands with each of them. Unused to being welcomed with such evident enthusiasm when they arrived nearly three hours late, the men mumbled apologies for their tardiness. 'It's the traffic down here, it's unbelievable', the driver moaned.

The door of number thirty-two opened and Sarah Notes, wearing denim jeans and a paint-flecked man's shirt, stood on the doorstep. She watched her husband discussing the pros and cons of the North Circular road with the men. Phrases like 'may as well be a car park' drifted over to her. She sighed. Geoff, stamping his feet to keep them warm in the late January afternoon, seemed genuinely interested in the trials and tribulations of the furniture removing business.

'I'll put the kettle on,' she called out. 'Why don't you start bringing stuff in?' If things didn't get moving fast she knew she would be up all night unpacking the bare necessities for their first night in their new home. Not for the first time she wondered at her husband's capacity for distraction from the task at hand. He had spent the last three hours slapping white paint over the hideous wallpaper in the living room and peering out of the window impatiently awaiting the arrival of the removal van with the contents of their former home in Yorkshire.

'I just want to get on with it.' he had said.

As Sarah made her way along the hallway to the kitchen at the back of the house she mentally thanked her mother for the loan of the electric kettle and a fresh pint of milk. She and Geoff had spent the last four days staying at her parents' home in Wimbledon. It had been a brief respite from the trauma of up-rooting from the little community of Gospel End and moving south. But now the lull was over. Geoff's new appointment was confirmed and he was expected to take up his responsibilities almost immediately.

Sarah filled the kettle and plugged it in. She dropped tea bags into mugs and waited for the water to boil. Down the hall she could hear Geoff welcoming the removal men to the house. 'Our first visitors,' she thought.

The living room was swathed in sheets. The removal men and Geoff sat perched on the edge of the tea chests they had just carried in and took stock of the situation. The van could be unloaded in a little over two hours if they really got a move on. The sooner it was done the sooner the men could get off home. They lit up cigarettes and waited for the tea to arrive.

'Are you sure about this?' one of the men asked Sarah as she entered, balancing the teas on top of a tin of biscuits.

'Sure of what?'

'Sure about moving here.' He looked around the living room. 'I mean, you had a nice place up north, didn't you? Bigger than this anyway. We all said how nice it was, didn't we lads?' His colleagues nodded agreement. 'What d'you want to come here for?'

'We didn't have a lot of say in the matter,' Geoff answered for Sarah. 'I have to go where my job takes me.'

'You ought to think about changing your job then. I wouldn't stand for giving up a decent place in the country to come here. There's hardly a blade of grass in sight.' He took a swig of tea.

'We're both from London originally, so it's like coming home for us. We'll soon get used to it again.' Geoff sounded almost apologetic.

The driver turned to his companions and chuckled. 'I mean, if there's any chance of you changing your mind, I'd rather you did it before we unloaded.'

'No, there's absolutely no chance of that.' For a moment it was unclear who Geoff was talking to, the men or Sarah who stood watching from the door.

'In that case we'd better be getting on with it. Any chance of a top up, love?' Sarah nodded curtly and exited the room.

Back in the kitchen she held tightly to the edge of the sink and sighed deeply. We should have stayed there, she thought. We should have fought the church authorities. They have no right to treat us like this. We don't deserve it. As she plugged the kettle in again her mind raced back to Gospel End. A glance at the clock told her that it would be milking time soon. John Selhurst would be preparing for the arduous ritual he performed twice daily, rain or shine. Jenny Drifford would no doubt be arriving back from wherever her sales trip had taken her today. For a few seconds she considered phoning Jenny, but it wasn't yet six o'clock and it would be a long distance call. A very long distance. The kettle reached boiling point and automatically clicked off.

Geoff knew, of course, that Sarah resented the move. He understood her frustration at leaving a work that was just beginning to flower. But it couldn't be helped. Geoff would miss the friends he had made in the all too brief months he had been at Gospel End. He would miss the darts team and he would especially miss helping to establish the once stagnant congregation in their new home in the worship centre. But, for Geoff, moving around the country was part of the job. It never really occurred to him that Sarah would see things any differently. She had known what to expect when she had married him. He knew that his wife missed her friends, but he didn't understand the pain she felt, nor the anger that dwelt within her, deep down.

It had been a shock when he had found himself in the sticks. Both Sarah and he had longed for a posting in London. As far as Geoff was concerned, this was God answering a prayer he had prayed many times at college. And now, with valuable lessons learned at Gospel End, he was back on course with the ministry he had always imagined himself in, an inner city one.

When, at last, the second mugs of tea were finished, and cigarettes were stubbed out on a paint pot lid which served as a hastily improvised ashtray, the men started to unload the van. Geoff cheerfully set to helping them. It had even stopped drizzling.

In the kitchen Sarah was rinsing the mugs out when the phone rang. It rang with a shrill business-like tone, and for a few seconds Sarah wondered what it was. The phone at Gospel End had seemed somehow friendlier with its old fashioned bell. The sound was coming from the bottom of the stairs and so she picked her way along the hall avoiding the packing cases that were being stacked inconveniently against the wall.

'Sarah Notes, can I help you?'

'Hello, can I speak to the Methodist minister please?'

'Hang on a second, I'll try and find him for you.' She placed the receiver on the stairs and went to the door. Geoff was making his way up the short path carrying a couple of dining room chairs.

'Phone for you.'

Geoff handed her the chairs and sat on the stairs

to take his call. After a few moments Sarah heard him hang up and call for her.

'Darling, where's that red file? The one with all the church details in it. There's an emergency down at the hospital and they want me to come straight away. The only trouble is, I have no idea where the hospital is.'

'You can't go out now. I can't cope with all this,' she indicated the ever growing pile of boxes and furniture. 'You don't start work for another week yet. Surely someone else could go?'

'They asked for me. Oh, I know, it's in that stack next to the bookcase in my study.' He turned and went to look.

'Where do you want these, love?' one of the men asked as he held a precariously balanced stack of boxes.

'Over there, in the corner. Please be careful, that's our best dinner service.' Sarah left the room to follow Geoff. She was just in time to see him dashing out of the house, red file in hand. 'Geoff,' she shouted, 'what time will you be back?'

'I'll see you when I see you,' he shouted back over the noise of a passing bus. She watched him get into the car and start the reluctant engine. As he pulled out into the flow of traffic she turned and went back inside. No kiss on the cheek, not even a goodbye. All he could see was the urgency of his mission.

Geoff clutched an A to Z street map as he guided the car through the maze of roads to the hospital. This was going to be his area, his patch. Soon he would know it like the back of his hand. He felt a wave of exhilaration. From tower blocks to the Victorian terraces, from the twee new designer apartments occupied by up and coming city whiz-kids to the virtual slums rife with social problems and needs, it was all his. A daunting challenge, yes, but his mind raced with the possibilities of the situation.

He had to brake hard as a group of children ran out in front of him. One of them, a black kid about thirteen, made an obscene gesture at him, as if it was Geoff's fault they had nearly been run over. Slightly shaken, Geoff drove the rest of the way to the hospital with his mind more on the road than on planning the future of his new parish.

The hospital building was a huge grey concrete and glass monstrosity. Bright sodium lamps lit the exterior and were reflecting on the damp concourse as Geoff hurried into the emergency department. Quickly he made his way to reception and announced his arrival. The receptionist looked suspiciously at the young man with spots of white emulsion in his hair. How could anyone so young be a member of the clergy? And where was his dog collar? She called to a porter and asked him to escort the minister to the intensive care ward. She didn't want him wandering around alone. You couldn't be too careful.

The ward sister was a smart blond woman who looked at him for a moment in incredulity.

'You are the minister from the church, then?' she said in a guttural South African accent. 'I'm sorry to have had to interrupt your decorating.'

For the first time Geoff realised what he must look like. He was wearing jeans and a dirty sweatshirt under an old anorak. He had speckles of paint on his hands and in his hair. He looked a mess. Acutely aware of this in the sterile hospital environment he smiled nervously.

'I'm Geoffrey Notes. The Reverend Geoffrey Notes, in fact. I've only just arrived. I wasn't expecting to be working tonight. My wife and I were unpacking and decorating. I'm sorry, I should have changed.'

The nurse smiled sympathetically. 'I quite understand,' she said.

'I was told there was an emergency.'

'Yes, I'm afraid that is so. We have a member of your church here. The mother has asked for the minister. I'll take you through.'

She led him towards two plastic flaps which, though transparent, revealed nothing more than a blur beyond. She held one of them open and Geoff walked in. He was totally unprepared for what filled the small cubicle.

First there was the array of machinery which seemed to occupy every available space. Monitors, dials, lights and cables. It was stacked on either side of the bed, and even suspended above it.

Then his eyes fixed on the small black face on the pure white sheet. The head was shaven, and a large wad of bandages covered part of the forehead and his left eye. There were signs of heavy bruising all over the face. It was the face of a child aged eight or nine.

Seated in a chair was the child's mother, her face tense and grim. Her eyes were wide with fear, fixed on her young son, willing him to live. She did not look up or greet the minister. She seemed totally unaware of his presence.

The ward sister pointed to the chair on the other side of the bed and Geoff slid past the electronic life support system and sat staring at mother and child. The ward sister left, and the not quite transparent flap folded back behind her. Geoffrey Notes suddenly felt very alone.

The thick smell of hospital disinfectant filled each breath and made his throat feel dry. He wanted to cough, but he dared not disturb the young woman who sat opposite. She was young, no older than himself. Her hair was plaited in many tight cords which were pulled back into a small bun on the back of her head. She wore a blue cardigan which she held closed as if against the cold.

Geoff sat and listened to the awful rhythm of the respirator. First a long, low sucking noise... then silence for just a second... a click... and then the whoosh of exhalation. The whole process repeated endlessly. And, matching the rhythm, the boy's chest rose and fell accordingly. It was a macabre setting, as the three of them waited together in the shadowland between life and death. There was nothing appropriate Geoff could do or say, so he just sat and watched and prayed.

Sarah Notes had about reached her limit with the three Yorkshire-men. Their preoccupation with the journey home irritated her beyond words. They had no particular interest where things were dumped. Their basic principle was that if it was off their lorry and inside the house the rest was up to her.

Boxes clearly marked 'Kitchen' were piled neatly in the upstairs bathroom, plastic sacks full of bed-linen had been stuffed into the store room under the stairs. Had she not protested, the large double wardrobe would have come to a permanent rest in the hallway because none of the three tired removal men relished the thought of heaving it step by step up the staircase. Even when they finally did so, they managed to score a neat line across the paintwork.

The whole process took far longer than anticipated due to frequent tea and cigarette breaks. During these times the men would discuss in painstaking detail the best route home. Sarah felt she knew the A1 well enough to have answered questions on 'Mastermind' by the time they had finished.

It was ten o'clock at night and very dark when they closed the door for the last time, and hauled themselves up into their lorry for the keenly anticipated journey northwards. Sarah watched them go from the living room window. She finished hanging the full length deep blue curtains above the large sash window and looked out into her new garden. It was a strip of land barely ten feet deep running the width of the terraced house. A low wall defined the boundary with the pavement, and there was a small unkempt flower bed beside it. Rather overgrown bushes grew close to the window. Sarah drew the curtains and realised she was all alone in the house at last. Geoff had been gone nearly five hours and she had not heard a word from him.

If I hadn't been roped into that stupid university rag week bed push I wouldn't have met Geoffrey Notes, she thought. I wouldn't have met him and so I couldn't have married him which means I wouldn't be here. If I wasn't here I'd be somewhere else and that would be just fine by me. I expect that wherever else I might have ended up it would be warmer than it is in here.

She went to look at the central heating boiler in the kitchen. It took twenty minutes to light the pilot and to find a setting that would allow for both heating and hot water. Suddenly she felt very tired. Time for a cup of drinking chocolate and bed. The drinking chocolate could be anywhere. The first place to look was in the bathroom. Amazingly she was right first time.

As she sat on the edge of the bed sipping from the steaming mug she began for the first time to feel slightly anxious about Geoff. She pictured him wandering lost in the maze of London streets. No, that was silly, he had a map. Perhaps the car had broken down. It had been making unhealthy noises on the drive down from Yorkshire. But no, they were members of the A.A. and anyway, Geoff would have telephoned. Maybe he had been mugged. Well, you never knew, not in London. Perhaps she should ring the hospital. 'Stop it' she told herself. 'Something has come up, that's all. You're just being silly.'

From downstairs came a scratching sound. Sarah strained to hear if the noise would repeat itself. Nothing. Cautiously she crept down the stairs. The house seemed empty. Sarah stood absolutely still in the hallway, listening. Still nothing. She could hear her heart beating in her chest. Suddenly there was another scratching sound. Had it come from the living room? Sarah stood rooted to the spot for a full two minutes. Nothing more was heard. Holding her breath she moved to the living room door. Very,

very slowly she pushed it open and switched the light on. The room was completely empty. She let her breath out in one long whoosh and relaxed. Then she almost leapt out of her skin as a tapping noise came from behind the curtains. Grabbing a broom that had been left against the wall she stabbed the curtains vigorously with its handle.

Chapter Two

Geoff Notes jerked awake as his head fell forward and he slumped in his chair. The dull rhythm of the life support system and the overpowering heat of the hospital ward had lulled him into a kind of stupor. His eyes felt like lead, and drowsiness swept over him in waves. He shuffled in his chair and tried to find a comfortable position. The mother opposite still showed no signs of being aware of his presence. Geoff realised that she was murmuring something in a voice barely louder than her breathing. He lent forward to hear better.

'Jesus, Jesus, Jesus,' over and over. Satisfied that she wasn't asking him to do something, but frustrated at his inability to do anything to relieve the suffering that hung as tangible as the smell of disinfectant, Geoff tried to relax. His eyes felt heavy again, and so he closed them for a moment.

He awoke sharply with the sound of an alarm. One of the monitors was flashing a red light, and the small cubicle was soon filled with doctors and nurses. Both he and the young black woman were escorted politely, but firmly, into a waiting room at the end of the corridor.

They sat beside each other looking down at the green carpet at their feet. 'I'm the Methodist minister, Geoff Notes. I'm so sorry.'

The young woman turned, as though to say something, then stared back at the floor.

'Is there anything you need?' Even as he spoke them, the words sounded empty.

'No, I'm okay', she whispered.

'What's his name?'

'Ben, he's only eight.' Tears began rolling down her cheeks, but she made no sound. Eventually she took out a white lace handkerchief and dabbed at her eyes. 'He only had the bike at Christmas.'

Geoff reached over and awkwardly held her hand. She gripped it tight, and drew strength from him. They sat like that for a long time, and no words were necessary.

Half an hour passed before the blonde sister entered to say that the immediate danger had passed. She led them back to the cubicle where they sat on opposite sides of the bed again, watching the little one.

'Thank you for coming, Mr Notes,' her voice snapped Geoff out of his day-dream. 'Ben and me, we belong to the church, you see.'

'Been going long?'

'Ever since my fella left, about three years ago. They've been nice to us there. Are you the new one then?'

'Yes, we've only just moved in. We've come from Yorkshire, my wife Sarah and me.' He smiled.

'I'm glad you came.'

'I've never felt so useless in my life.'

'I'm still glad you came.'

They lapsed back into silence. But now they were silent together, a bond having been formed. Two people facing the unfaceable, never speaking the question which filled their hearts with terror. Will Ben live?

Cautiously Sarah peeked behind the curtains, half expecting a monster to leap out at her. There was nothing there. Only one of the thin branches on the bush outside tapping the window. Sarah's relief was so great she sank to the floor and sat there shaking. When at last she could stand up again she went into the kitchen and grabbed a bread knife and went outside to tackle the offending branch. Anyone watching would have been surprised to see a young woman viciously attacking a bush with a large knife. The serrated edge eventually cut through the limb and Sarah triumphantly carried both it and the knife back inside.

Emotionally exhausted, Sarah headed upstairs to the bedroom again. The mug of drinking chocolate stood cold and only half drunk on the bedside cabinet. For the life of her, Sarah couldn't think where the bedding had been unloaded, so she rolled up a towel for a pillow and found her coat. Then she switched off the light and lay on the bed, pulling the coat over her. She closed her eyes and willed herself to sleep.

There were no curtains at the bedroom window, so each passing car's headlights traced strange shadows across the walls and ceiling. Even with her

eyes tight shut, Sarah was aware of them. The more
she wanted to sleep and pass the rest of this dreadful night in unconsciousness, the less likely it
seemed she would.

A dull thudding came from outside. It seemed to
get louder by the minute. Sarah tried to ignore it.
For what seemed like eternity she lay there in that
state between wakefulness and the blessed release of
sleep. At first she was too tired to move. Whatever
it was would go away. No one played music that
loud at this time of night. The red digital numbers
on her bedside alarm clock flicked towards half past
midnight.

The sound of shouting and laughter pulled her
back from the brink of sleep. She sat up and threw
the coat to the floor, then got up and approached
the window. Every room in the house opposite was
ablaze with light, and full of people. They were
dancing. Even from this distance and with the window closed Sarah could make out that the stereo
system was blasting out a tune that had recently
been in the charts. She hadn't liked it then, either.
With horror Sarah realised that the party was only
just starting. This was no suburban 'cheese and
wine' affair, this was a full blown disco... and the
clientele looked rough.

Gradually, the lights in the other houses were
going on, one by one, and anxious faces were peering out into the darkness. Sarah looked down as the
door at number twenty eight opened wide, and a
fierce looking man in a purple dressing gown strode
over the road and shouted abuse into the open door
to the dancers beyond.

Three angry men came out, obviously the worse

for drink, and surrounded the man. Obscenities flew thick and fast, and within seconds the man in the dressing gown was being pushed back and forth between the three drunks. Suddenly a fight erupted, Sarah watched horrified as the man was kicked and beaten. Other people poured out from the party and from other houses in the street as a free-for-all developed. Who was trying to stop the fight and who was participating became impossible to discern. It was with great relief that she heard a police siren wailing in the distance. Sarah turned from the window and climbed back onto the bed, then lay staring at the ceiling. A blue flashing light stabbed the darkness, and other sirens drew nearer. She turned over, covered herself with the thick warm coat, and sobbed. Was this a nightmare, or was it for real?

She awoke to the unfamiliar drone of the rush hour traffic crawling past the house. It was 8:15 am, and she turned over to find Geoff asleep beside her. He had silently manoeuvred his way past the piles of packing cases and, like Sarah, was lying under his coat. She lay there for a long while, looking at the ashen, strained face of the man she loved. Even as he slept she could sense how tired and drained he was.

What was it about him that she liked so much? Even when she was totally exasperated with him, she felt a warmth towards him which was too deep to define. She looked back over their brief three and a half year marriage; she pictured the cramped student flat at theological college in Bristol, the large old manse at Gospel End, and now their squat

London terraced house. You couldn't say they were in a rut.

The strain and disappointment of the work at Gospel End had taken its toll on Geoff. She could tell that much of his raw enthusiasm and naivety about the ministry had gone, rubbed away on the grind stone of experience. In a way he was less confident, yet more mature and more dependent on God than ever before. She leant across, kissed him gently on the forehead and whispered.

'Welcome home, Geoffrey Notes, you naughty stop-out.'

His reply was stilted, spoken from the depths of sleep. 'Sorry love. It was bad. A kid run over. They don't know if he'll make it...' He rolled over and went back to sleep, and Sarah held him tight. He was warm, and secure.

At nine o'clock, Miss Briggs, or Ms Briggs as she preferred to be called, walked up the terrace to number thirty-two to welcome the new incumbent and his wife. It was most unusual for her to make use of the flexitime arrangement which was available in her office. A woman of pattern and procedure she always caught the 8:24 from Redbrook to Victoria, and enjoyed a leisurely twelve minute walk down Victoria Street to her office, an annex of the Department of Trade and Industry, the DTI. Assuming the train ran on time and wasn't delayed by various natural phenomena like snow or leaves, she would normally have time for a quick cup of coffee before starting work at precisely 9 am. But on this occasion, in her role as senior steward of Redbrook Methodist Church, she felt beholden to welcome the 'new man'.

She paused to admire the exterior paintwork at number thirty-two, a job recently completed in honour of the new minister's arrival, then tapped the door knocker smartly. There was no reply. Funny, surely he was not out performing his duties already. She gave the knocker another couple of taps, more vigorously this time. It was as she turned to go that the door swung open revealing a bedraggled Geoff Notes. His hair was unbrushed, his face unshaven, and he was rubbing sleep from his eyes.

'Yes, can I help you?' He looked puzzled and disorientated, as if he was not quite sure where he was nor what he was doing there.

'Good morning, I'm Ms Briggs, your senior steward at the church,' she said heartily. 'I'm sorry if I disturbed you, but I thought I'd call in on you on my way to work to see if you need anything.'

Geoff refrained from muttering 'only some more sleep,' and welcomed the smartly dressed middle-aged woman into the house. The whole place was in chaos. There were boxes everywhere as well as ladders and paint. Furniture was placed where it clearly didn't fit. A large twig was stuck in a vase on the kitchen table.

Ms Briggs perched herself on a bar-stool in the kitchen and gladly accepted the offer of a cup of coffee. After washing up some mugs from the previous day, Geoff proceeded to hunt for the jar of coffee. After failing to locate it he suggested that she might like to try tea. Ms Briggs declined, and said she'd go without.

Sarah entered the kitchen with slightly more

composure, and was introduced to the visitor. 'You
don't know where the coffee is, do you, darling?'

'Yes, of course, I'll go and get it. It's in the
bathroom.'

Ms Briggs looked puzzled, but seemed relieved
that her morning infusion of caffeine would soon be
forthcoming. 'Now, down to business, Geoff...
we're really pleased that you're here, and we're sure
you are going to heal the rift quickly.'

'Rift, what rift?'

Ms Briggs looked startled. 'No-one told you
then?'

'No, I was just sent. A week ago I was in Yorkshire.'

'Well, we've been without a minister for about a
year and a half now, because inner London isn't
everyone's cup of tea.'

'And...' Geoff prompted. He was becoming a
little impatient.

'Well, there are the radicals and there are the
charismatics, and never the twain shall meet
except, of course, at the church council.' She smiled
as sweetly as she knew how.

'And you, do you represent any particular
group?'

'No, no, you're quite safe with me. I've been a
civil servant for nearly thirty years: I'm bred for
impartiality. That's why they made me the senior
steward. I don't think any of them are right. I'm
just a good old Methodist.'

Geoff's heart sank. He'd had enough of good old
Methodists in Gospel End. A title like that could
cover a multitude of agendas. 'And is there anything you should warn me about?'

'My advice is simple. Bide your time, Geoffrey. Don't choose sides too quickly. Let them all think you are on their side, at least for the time being. I'm sure you'll win them round.'

And with that she took a first sip of coffee. It was Sarah's special 'Cambodian Workers'' brew that made a political point rather than a drinkable cup. Ms Briggs sipped again, and again. But she waited in vain for the surge of caffeine for which her body craved.

Ms Briggs left number thirty-two, and briskly walked towards the station to catch the 9:24, her task complete. On the way she passed a zebra crossing and a yellow police notice which asked for witnesses to a road traffic accident involving a child.

Back at the manse Sarah and Geoff started on the long hard slog of unpacking and turning a house into a home. No one else called on them, either from the neighbouring houses or from the church. They assumed they were being given 'space' to settle in.

For the next three days life was one long round of painting and stacking things in cupboards and on shelves. Geoff made frequent visits to the hospital to see Ben and Miriam, his mother. She was sleeping on a camp bed in a room a few yards down the corridor from where her son lay unconscious, kept alive by respirators and high technology.

They lived on take-away food; pre-packed plastic tasting sandwiches at lunchtime and a curry or Chinese meal for supper. Neither had enough energy to think about shopping or cooking. Gradually the house was restored to some semblance of normality as tea chests were emptied and stacked in the back garden and furniture was placed into position.

It was ten o'clock on the fourth night when the doorknocker thudded loudly. Geoff was standing in the hall drilling a hole with an electric drill.

'Coming... just a minute.' He shouted, finishing off the hole which would eventually contain a picture hook. From this prestigious place would hang a large framed canvas depicting the Fox and Hounds, the pub which had meant so much to Geoff at Gospel End. The drill whined to a stop and he went to open the front door.

On the doorstep stood a scrawny looking girl with jet black hair, dark purple lipstick and a kind of pallid face make-up which made her look like death. She was dressed in a leather jacket several sizes too large for her which had obviously seen better days, and tight black trousers. It was difficult to estimate her age, but Geoff guessed about nineteen.

'Hello, can I help you?' he asked.

'I doubt it, but I gotta try, ain't I?' the girl responded unenthusiastically.

Rosie, as she was called, sat on the sofa and warmed her hands on the coffee mug. Geoff was seated in the armchair and Sarah sat cross-legged on the floor looking up at their visitor. Both Geoff and Sarah were glad to see someone... anyone!

'There's been some hassle over at our place. We live at number twenty-seven, opposite.' The girl took out a cigarette and lit it slowly, puffing smoke into the air before continuing. 'There was this fight, okay, the other night. Nothing much really, but the police want to make a big thing of it.'

'Oh yes, during the party, you mean?'

'What party?' Geoff looked nonplussed.

'The first night, when you were at the hospital.' Sarah turned back to Rosie and tried to look sympathetic. It would be a long time before she forgot that particular night.

'Well, they say we started it, and we didn't. First thing I knew about it was the Bill coming and dragging my Dave away. I just wondered if you saw anything? We could do with a witness.' Rosie flicked ash into her empty coffee mug, and Sarah tried not to show her displeasure.

'Would you like an ashtray?'

'Nah, this'll do. Well, did you see anything?'

'I heard the noise of the party and went to the window to see what was going on. Then I saw a man in a dressing gown from next door go over and tell you to shut up. Three of your friends came out and there was some arguing.' Sarah paused, as if trying to remember. She replayed the scene in her head, the pushing and shouting, and then the hitting and kicking.

'But who started it? Did you see the man in the dressing gown hit my Dave?' Rosie was leaning forward, her eyes pleading with Sarah to give the right answer.

'I'm sorry, Rosie, but it wasn't that man who threw the first punch, it was one of the others.' She saw the look of disappointment in the girl's face. Wanting to give some grounds for hope, Sarah added, 'but I couldn't say which of the three it was. It all happened too fast, and it was dark of course.'

Rosie stubbed the cigarette out in the bottom of the mug. A thin streak of smoke rose from it as she did so. 'Oh well, I didn't expect any help. Not from round here.' She placed the mug down by her feet.

'I'd like to have helped, but I can only tell you what I saw. I'm sorry if it's not what you wanted to hear. Is there anything else we can do for you?' Sarah was curious to learn more about this white faced lady.

'A bath would be nice, the 'leccy's off over at our place.' Rosie stood to leave. 'But I don't 'spect you want people like me traipsing through your house.'

'Of course you can have a bath. The water's hot, why not have one now? I'll get you a towel.' Sarah got up. Rosie shrugged her shoulders as if in agreement, and meekly followed her upstairs to the bathroom.

Geoff, left alone, picked up the TV remote control and flicked through the channels. He just caught the closing news headlines and was soon engrossed in a thriller set in Berlin before the cold war thawed. He smiled to himself, and found it vaguely comforting. Whatever twists and turns the plot had in store the ending was already determined, written into history. During a commercial break he went upstairs to see where Sarah was and found the bathroom empty. The bedroom door was closed, but he could hear quiet talking from within. He hesitated for a moment and then decided to leave them be. As he crept back downstairs he heard sobbing.

The film was coming to its exciting, if bloody, conclusion when he heard the front door click and Sarah re-entered the room. She sat at his feet and, without taking his eyes from the screen, he ran his hands through her thick dark hair and then gave her scalp a massage. 'So, we've opened a bath house now, have we?'

'She didn't have time for a bath. She's coming back tomorrow.'

'What gives then? You were nattering long enough.' Geoff moved his hands down to his wife's shoulders and neck and continued to massage her gently. The knots in her muscles began to relax. She leant back against him and sighed contentedly.

'You missed your vocation, you did.'

'Well?' Geoff prompted.

'I don't think you need to know. It was just girl talk. Anyway, most of the time she was just crying.'

'Are you sure I don't need to know?'

'Absolutely. Left a bit, darling, wonderful,' Sarah was being evasive. She turned and kissed his knee.

'Sarah Notes, sometimes you can be so exasperating...'

She smiled up at him. 'Touché. Now shut up and keep massaging. I want to find out what happened in the good old bad old days, before the wall came tumbling down.'

Chapter Three

On the first Sunday of his ministry at Redbrook, Geoffrey Notes stood in the minister's vestry feeling nervous. He was very apprehensive about meeting his new congregation for the first time, and Ms Briggs, the senior steward, didn't exactly have the ability to put a minister at ease.

'Well Mr Notes, it's one minute to eleven,' she said, looking at her chunky digital watch, 'and I feel that we should pause for prayer.'

Geoff obediently bowed his head. He imagined that Ms Briggs prayed to the Almighty with the hushed respect with which she spoke to her superiors in the hierarchy of the Civil Service. Her language was precise and carefully formed, and was reminiscent of an internal D.T.I. memo.

'Almighty and Everlasting Father, Prince of Peace, King of Kings. You see all things, know all things and understand all things. We commit our service to you, and commend our new minister to you. In the Name of Christ our Saviour. Amen.'

Geoff felt like adding, 'I would be obliged if you would take action on this matter at your earliest convenience.'

Geoff entered the bright, carpeted sanctuary of Redbrook Methodist church and stood at the lectern surveying his new church. Although the building would never win any prizes for architecture, he had to admit that it was a lot more practical than the previous chapel at Gospel End. Rows of light pine chairs with blue padded seats and back rests were laid out before him. The back of the church had a large window that allowed him to see the entrance foyer. Beneath the window was a table with a display of books laid out on it. The sanctuary end at the front of the church had a much lower roof than the rest of the building and this section was only about twenty feet square. Dominating the church was a modern stained glass window, which to Geoff's untutored eye held no readily apparent symbolism or meaning. It had dark blue glass punctuated with patches of light blue glass, a yellow lightning flash streaked from top to bottom and a text 'Where Sheep May Safely Graze' was written in gothic script in a panel at its base. The whole building had a bright airy feeling about it, and Geoff stood enjoying the general mayhem before him. About half of the congregation had not noticed his grand entrance, and they were standing in groups all around the hundred seat auditorium.

There was a loud buzz of conversation. People were embracing and greeting one another, and someone was laughing very loudly. Two little black boys were playing tag up and down the central aisle.

Several young people were at the front of the church trying to get a p.a. system working, and one young man with a long pony tail was busily engaged in erecting a very large drum kit, complete with cymbals.

Ms Briggs cleared her throat and snapped, 'Please, please, calm down everyone. It's time for the service to start. Please return to your seats.' There was a general murmur of agreement, and gradually the assembled throng of about eighty people filled the rows of chairs.

During the singing of the first hymn 'God is love' which Geoff had picked for its breadth of appeal and no-nonsense message, he surveyed the congregation in front of him. There was a free and easy atmosphere, and a sense of joy in the air that he quite liked.

He scanned the faces of the people before him. Now and again his eye would come to rest on someone, and even as he sang, he asked God's blessing on them. In a matter of seconds he was quite overcome with emotion: he felt a sense of bonding and of belonging to this group of strangers, which startled him. It was as if, even now, he loved this strange mix of black and white, old and young, rich and poor who were to be his London flock.

There was a very large West Indian man with a black moustache, whose booming bass voice sang out over the rest of the congregation. But he was singing with faith, and his eyes sparkled with the love of which he sang.

The young couple in the front row were obviously quite affluent. His immaculate pin-striped suit and her beautifully tailored maroon outfit spoke of success and money. They stood close together, sharing the same hymn book and expressing in their closeness to one another a deep affection.

The old man in the third row just stood and smiled. Geoff guessed that he was blind, but there was a glow in his face that spoke of joy, and of a quiet acceptance of the hardship which life had thrust upon him.

And of course, there was Sarah, giving him her knowing look. She knew just how nervous he was feeling at this new beginning in Redbrook. He was very glad that she was there.

Then, as the congregation launched enthusiastically into the third verse of the hymn, one of the rear doors of the church was pushed ajar and Ben's mother, Miriam, crept in. She sat in the back row and bowed her head in prayer. The hymn suddenly seemed so inappropriate, and Geoff wished he could stop the musicians and suggest an alternative.

'How happy is our portion here.
God is love! God is love!
His promises our spirits cheer.
God is love! God is love!

But he looked again, and Ben's mother was now on her feet and singing, a big beaming smile filling her face...

'He is our sun and shield by day,
By night he near our tents will stay,

He will be with us all the way—
God is love! God is love!

It was a great service. When he prayed, he felt
that his prayers were lifted by the faith of the
people, and when he preached, they drew the Word
from deep within him. It was a long service, and the
warm greetings and expressions of affection over
coffee afterwards took nearly an hour. Sarah felt
loved and welcomed. It was all so different from the
early days at Gospel End.

Geoff returned to the vestry to pick up his coat,
and found Ms Briggs sitting at the table counting
the collection and entering figures in a large ledger.
She was humming happily to herself, engrossed in
the task at hand. When she became aware of his
presence she looked up and beamed at him.

'Well done, Mr Notes. A good first service, I
thought,' she said, quite genuinely.

'Thank you. But tell me, what's all this about a
split church? If it is split, I couldn't see the join!'

Ms Briggs put down her fountain pen, placed
blotting paper over the rows of newly entered figures and looked up at him sympathetically.

'Well, you've only met half the congregation this
morning, Mr Notes. The other half come tonight. I
think you'll need a slightly more, um,' she hesitated, as if trying to find a diplomatic word, 'well,
more intellectual approach.'

'You mean that there are two congregations
here?' Geoff stared at her in disbelief.

'Well, you could describe it like that'.

'And don't they ever meet?' Geoff stuttered in
disbelief.

'Oh yes, of course; they meet at the church council. It's on Wednesday.'

Geoff shook his head and sighed. He pulled on his coat and sauntered silently out of the church to where Sarah was waiting. They walked, hand in hand, up the busy street towards the manse. A group of some ten or twelve boys aged between nine and fourteen loitered on one of the corners. Some of them kicked a can back and forth between them, while others just stood and chatted. Sarah was concerned to see that three or four of them were smoking, including a couple of the very youngest. As they walked past the group the boys went silent, the can kicking stopped, and all of them simply stared at Geoff and Sarah. It was an intimidating experience although there was no hint of danger. As they proceeded further up the road they heard the clattering of the can again.

After lunch Geoff was called back to the hospital to see young Ben. His mother, Miriam, sat in her usual chair by his bedside. She stood up to greet Geoff.

'Thanks for coming,' she said, 'only the doctor wants to see me this afternoon, and I didn't want to see him on my own.'

'No problem,' whispered Geoff, as he took his usual chair beside the awful respirator. He could discern not the slightest change in young Ben's condition. The bruising may have faded a little but his face was cast in unnatural stillness.

A few minutes later Miriam and Geoff were shown into the sister's office, where a dark suited gentleman was sitting leafing through a pile of reports.

'Ah, do come in.' He stood politely, and motioned towards two chairs in front of the desk, 'could you arrange a cup of tea, Sister?'

The sister nodded knowingly, and closed the door gently behind her. Geoff already had a strong suspicion that what they were about to hear was not good news.

The consultant neurologist leafed through the papers some more, as if looking for some important document. In fact, he was composing himself.

'The truth is' he put the papers down at last and looked straight into Miriam's eyes, 'that Ben is not responding well. He is in a deep coma. We all hoped that by now there would have been some response, but as yet, there's no way we can take him off the respirator.'

Geoff reached over and gripped Miriam's hand. He knew that the consultant was reaching for words, and he wanted to help him.

'Does there come a point at which it might be necessary to turn the respirator off?' Geoff could hardly believe what he was saying.

'Yes, I'm afraid so,' said the doctor, his eyes still fixed on Miriam. 'Decisions like this are never easy, and obviously we wouldn't do that until we'd exhausted every possibility. But we'd want both of you involved in that decision, if it had to be made.'

'No, not yet. Not ever,' said Miriam firmly. 'It mustn't be turned off.'

'No, of course not. Not yet,' said the doctor, firmly, closing the file. The sister looked through the office window, and, when the doctor nodded, she entered with a tray of tea. Almost immediately both the doctor and the ward Sister said their good-byes and left. Times like this weren't easy for any-one, even hardened medical staff.

Miriam turned to Geoff, 'It looks like it's up to God to do something now.'

Geoff, completely taken aback by the firm way in which Miriam spoke, nodded silently in agreement.

'Will you call the church to prayer?' Her eyes were wet with tears.

'Yes, we'll all pray together. I'll start asking them tonight,' he said softly, and, without pausing, he closed his eyes and began to pray. 'Father, we cry out to you for little Ben. We ask that you would pour your healing power down upon him, and bring him back from the depths of unconsciousness. For Jesus' sake. Amen.' She gripped his hand tight.

At 6:15 that evening Ms Briggs unlocked her domain, the minister's vestry, and hung up her coat on the peg provided. The room contained a desk and three upright wooden chairs. On the walls were a number of black and white photographs of previous ministers and a mirror. Beside the desk was a small bookcase. She sat and flicked through a 'Book of vestry prayers' in the hope of finding something appropriate for a new minister.

Geoff arrived a few moments later. He was feeling sensitive and low as a result of his afternoon at the hospital. He placed the sheet of paper containing his neatly typed 'Order of service' gently on the vestry table, 'I hope this will fit the bill,' he smiled.

'An order of service? Didn't I explain? I'm so sorry, Mr Notes. We don't need an order of service tonight. It's more of a discussion group.'

'A discussion group?' Geoff was wide eyed, 'you mean I haven't got to preach?'

'Oh no, there's nothing like that. We just sit in a circle and talk.'

'Oh'. Geoff was wearing his nonplussed expression again. Ms Briggs prayed her vestry prayer and led him into the church. In one corner of the room a space had been cleared and about fifteen chairs had been placed in a circle. People were chatting loudly, and there were just two seats left; one for him, and one for Ms Briggs.

A very tall man in a bright green pullover with a great sweep of hair which he kept pushing back out of his eyes seemed to be in charge of the group. 'Welcome Geoff, I'm Pete. We're so pleased you could join us tonight. Please feel free to make whatever contribution you wish to the group; and we're also glad to see you, Sarah. You're among friends here.'

Geoff and Sarah smiled and nodded approvingly, wondering what was going to happen next. Pete leant forward, brushed back his hair, clasped his hands together and launched enthusiastically into his introduction.

'Our text tonight is from the Chief Justice of California who said, and I quote, 'We have probed the earth, excavated it, burned it, buried things in it... That does not fit my definition of a good tenant. If we were here on a month to month basis, we would have been evicted long ago.' Any comments, folks?'

A girl in her mid-twenties, with long blonde hair and a large anti-nuke badge, took up the theme. 'I blame it on the NIMBY mentality. If only people would take a wider view of things...'

Ms Briggs smiled, 'Excuse me dear, what's a Nimby mentality?'

'Not in my back yard, of course,' explained the girl. 'After all, we're the only species to be able to understand what is happening. We can help or hinder the system. It's our responsibility to treat the whole earth with respect.'

'Absolutely,' said the bald gentleman in the dark suit, who gazed through thick tinted spectacles. 'I think Giscard got it right when he campaigned on the ticket of "a more human kind of growth". He was both a modernist and a nostalgist, a believer in post-industrial Le Corbusian concepts of factories amid meadows, but also in conservation.'

Sarah had the distinct feeling that she'd been in this discussion long ago, in the manse at Gospel End, during her 'Green' period. Already her mind was full of concepts and ideas which she could air, but she restrained herself and only spoke briefly.

'We all live in the world. But there's also a world that lives in us. My view of the world is probably different from yours. This is because what I value in the world is different from what you find valuable. Essentially, the job of the environmentalist is to change the inscape, that undiscovered country of the mind.'

'Exactly,' chimed Geoff, seeing the opening which Sarah had neatly left for him. 'It's all summed up in the "Brother Sun and Sister Moon" thinking of Francis of Assisi. His view of the world was that if everything had been made by God, then everything he came across was sacred and ought to be respected. He didn't see humans as the supreme rulers of the universe—they weren't the top of the heap—they were one part of a big family which included the rest of creation. He saw God as Father and everything in creation as brother and sister. It's that kind of inscape thinking we need to cultivate.'

Peter leant forward, his hands clenched, and his hair covering his eyes. 'Mmm, interesting concept Geoff. But it doesn't give much inspiration to those who don't believe in God. Couldn't we get further in contemporary society by, for example, exploring the ancient Chinese view of the world summed up by Yin and Yang?'

There was a long pause. Geoff looked at Sarah and hid a mischievous smirk by covering his mouth with his hand. Ms Briggs was now completely lost.

'Perhaps you could briefly explain the theory,' said Ms Briggs helpfully,' I'm a bit rusty on it myself.' She was doing her best to earth the conversation.

'Yes, of course' Peter muttered, still clenching his fists and hidden under his hair. 'From the beginning of the universe, two forces have been in opposition to each other. One is called Yin and the other Yang. Yin is anything which is passive, cold, dark, black, receptive or below. But Yang is energy, warm, bright, red or above. When either Yin or Yang gets too strong for the other, then disaster, chaos and destruction threaten. Now whether we accept this literally or not, it is a useful metaphor for the need of balance in the universe.'

'Thank you so much, Peter,' Ms Briggs smiled, 'so clearly put, wasn't it Geoff?'

Geoff smiled in return. And so the conversation

continued, flowing freely but often at tangents. Frequently it consisted of complex statements which were hard to follow, and for a while it seemed as though God wasn't going to get a mention, but slowly the conversation worked its way around to the Christian response to these challenging issues. Geoff and Sarah found themselves being intellectually stretched in ways that they had seldom been since late night discussions at college. They realised that despite the occasionally pretentious language, here was a group of Christians who were deeply concerned for the world of which they were a part. They weren't satisfied with a 'quick fix' solution to global problems. They wanted carefully considered strategies mapped out, and the church to take a lead in healing a wounded planet. Sarah, in particular, was very excited. As the meeting drew to a close Geoff asked permission to make an announcement, and Peter nodded in agreement.

'Well, some of you will know that Ben, an eight year old in the Sunday school, was knocked down on his bike recently. Well, friends, it doesn't look good. He's on a respirator at the General, and unless something changes soon he might have to come off the respirator. His mother Miriam has asked if the whole church would turn to prayer this week. So, I'm proposing to meet here for an hour each morning at seven o'clock, and I'd be grateful if you could join me.'

The announcement obviously caused a degree of embarrassment, for, even while he was still speaking, various members of the group began to get up and put their coats on. Geoff would have liked to have led the meeting in prayer for Ben then, but it was clear that they were all anxious to leave.

Geoff and Sarah arrived home exhausted and confused. 'It's like having two churches Geoff, they're just so different. I don't see how you'll ever get them together. And why did they seem so unhappy with the prospect of a prayer meeting?'

'One thing's for sure,' Geoff smiled, 'I don't think that Yin and Yang are an established part of Methodist theology!'

The doorknocker thudded, and Geoff answered the door. It was Rosie, tears streaming down her face. 'Come in, love, what's the matter?'

By this time Sarah was already in the hall, and Rosie ran into her arms sobbing. 'They came tonight and arrested Dave, and the squat's been evicted. I've got nowhere to go.'

'Oh yes you have,' whispered Sarah, 'you can stay here until we can sort something out.'

Geoffrey Notes looked at his wife in astonishment. It seemed they'd not only opened a bathhouse, but a hostel, as well.

Chapter Four

Geoff Notes was already up and had gone out of the house by the time that Sarah got up the following morning. He had an early morning prayer meeting to attend. She was still feeling drained and exhausted after having talked to Rosie late into the night. Now she sat curled up on the lounge settee in her dressing gown with a steaming hot cup of coffee and the morning post.

Sarah had always enjoyed receiving letters, right from having three different pen-pals when she was a child. She took each envelope and always looked at the postmark and handwriting before opening it. Letters always held a kind of mystery for her, and she often felt she could guess whether the contents were good or bad, even before she opened them.

The first letter was formal, typed and sealed in a thick white envelope embossed with the words 'Cameron Publishing UK'. Her heart leapt when she saw it. It was from the company for whom she'd worked before the move to Yorkshire.

It was not good news. The letter from her old boss warmly welcomed her back to London but regretted that in the current economic climate the company would not be able to reinstate her as a desk editor. They would, they promised, keep her name on file. She'd so missed publishing, and having been away from the office for less than a year she had hoped that she could have returned to her career. Evidently, that was not to be, at least not immediately. As she re-folded the letter and inserted it back in its envelope Sarah tried hard not to feel disappointed. She sipped her coffee and indulged in a moment of self pity. She had given up so much to be with Geoff. What had she gained in return?

The other item of post only seemed to make matters worse. It was a 'Welcome to your new home' card with a picture of two squirrels peeking out of a tree trunk. It was from Sarah's best friend at Gospel End, Jenny Drifford, and contained only a brief message. 'We're all praying for you. I'm seeing John... it's getting serious. Phone soon. Loads of luv, Jenny.'

Sarah gripped the card tight and began to cry. It was the release of a great flood of emotion. The hurried departure from Gospel End, the painful farewells and the stress of the opening days at Redbrook, and now the further set back in her career... they had all taken their toll. To cap it all, this card reminded her again how much she missed Jenny. She lay prostrate on the large sofa and shook with emotion as tears flowed down her face.

Rosie stood by the door watching her for some

considerable time, and then, unable to restrain herself, quietly drifted to her side, sat on the floor, softly touched Sarah's back and whispered 'It's all right, love, I'm here.'

Meanwhile, Geoffrey Notes was negotiating with a particularly officious police Sergeant at the front counter of Redbrook Central Police Station. Geoff had worn his best suit and most orthodox looking dog-collar in the hope of gaining an interview with Dave Wilson from the squat at number twenty-seven.

At long last, after lengthy discussions in the back office with a detective and the custody officer, permission was granted for Geoff to have a special 'five minute' visit with the prisoner. Geoff followed the sergeant down the two stone flights of stairs, and was told that he could only speak to Dave through the small eye-grill in the door.

The footsteps of the custody sergeant echoed as he raced back up the stairs. Geoff was not left totally alone: a young PC stood silently at one end of the shadowy corridor watching him conduct his interview with the prisoner. What Geoff saw when he peered through the grill was a thin young man sat on the low platform that served as both seating and bed in the cell.

'Hi, Dave, we've not met. I live at number thirty-two, opposite you. I just came to say that Rosie's okay. She's staying with us for a while, and we'll take good care of her.'

'Are you the vicar, then?' Dave got up from the bed and came to the cell door, standing so close that all Geoff could see of him was his eyes.

'Yes, sort of.'

'I wondered if you could do me a favour?' The grey eyes peered out into the darkness, and strained to see what Geoffrey Notes was like.

'If I can.'

There was a long pause, and then the quiet voice pleaded, 'Will you speak for me in court this morning? If you explained that Rosie is pregnant, and that we're hoping to get married, I think it might help.'

'Rosie's pregnant? Are you sure?'

'Yes, ask your wife if you don't believe me... they've been talking about it.'

Geoff looked at the man, trying to guess whether he was speaking the truth. 'And are you positive about wanting to marry her? For love, I mean, rather than just for the baby?'

'Of course. You must believe me. All I want is to be with Rosie.'

Geoff, flushed with the drama of the situation and touched by the desperation in Dave's voice, sighed a sigh of complete frustration. Even on this brief meeting Dave Wilson didn't strike him as the most up front and reliable person he had ever met. But then the man was in a police cell and that might prejudice this first impression of his former neighbour. He didn't know what to do for the best.

Just then the echoing footsteps returned, but this time the custody sergeant was accompanied by Dave's 'brief' who was trying to read about the case as he walked.

And so, in the shadows of the custody cell corridor, Geoffrey Notes struck a deal with the young barrister and the prisoner. He would ask the court to 'bind Dave over' into his pastoral care and keeping, for the sake of Rosie and the unborn child.

On that same Monday morning Ms Briggs caught the 8:24 am to London, Victoria; made her brisk twelve minute walk down Victoria Street and sat drinking her early morning coffee while she waited for the arrival of the morning mail.

It was a routine she greatly enjoyed. In fact, her timetable within the Civil Service was the framework for her whole life. She'd never wanted to do anything else, even from her school days, and the slow climb through the ranks to her current position had been demanding but worthwhile.

In the complex pecking order of the Department of Trade and Industry she had risen high up in the ranks of seniority. She now qualified for her own office, secretarial help each morning, and 'office greenery' which consisted of a row of pot plants on her windowsill. She loved the view from the window, because on tiptoe, she could just see the walls of Westminster Abbey and the clock face of Big Ben. She was virtually at the centre of things, here in the D.T.I., and she felt needed.

The light flashed on her internal telephone, and she picked it up briskly. It was one minute after nine; a new week was beginning. 'Yes, yes of course... right away.' It was a call she'd been half expecting. Her heart raced with excitement. She put down the receiver and hurried along the corridor to Personnel. These had been unsettling months within the civil service; times were changing and departments were being reorganised. With reorganisation came opportunities for promotion. Ms Briggs had seniority over the two other people on her grade and now, at last, her time had come. She would be moving from this annex in Victoria to Whitehall, the centre of government.

Within ten minutes she was back, and was stood gazing out of her precious window, her whole world lying in pieces around her. The words of the personnel officer rang around her mind '...early retirement... redundancy... staff surplus...' She quickly scooped a few personal items into a plastic carrier bag and made her way along the tiled corridors with their myriad doors and hurried out into the street. She stood on the front step and gazed at the busy roar of traffic for just a moment, then turned, and walked briskly back to the station. There was no reason why she had to clear her office and leave so quickly, it was her choice. She had been given a month's notice, but since she was owed twenty three days leave she had determined to go immediately. Ms Briggs had no desire to see anyone, not just now, least of all any sympathetic colleagues.

As she walked up the busy pavement against the flow of young hopefuls on their way to work she suddenly felt that life was over. For the first time in her life she understood the meaning of the word 'redundant'. It seemed only yesterday that she was one of those 'young hopefuls' herself, beginning work at the Civil Service and setting out on the slow climb to the top.

But now, here she was, walking home on a Monday morning, her purpose gone, her ambitions shattered. Who would ever want to employ her again? How could she start out on something new at this time of life? No, she'd had her chances and she'd done her best. It was the end of her career, there could be no doubt about it. She felt very empty and light-headed. A doctor would have recognised the symptoms of shock.

Back at the manse the roles of Sarah and Rosie had completely reversed. Sarah, who had cast herself as the strong, dependable counsellor, was weeping on Rosie's shoulder—and the scrawny unkempt girl was listening sympathetically.

Sarah poured out the story of all that had happened at Gospel End, the disappointment of the move there, the isolation and loneliness she'd felt as a minister's wife, and the dramatic events leading to the demolition of the church. But she also spoke of the friends they'd made, of the dreams they'd dreamed, and of the life at Gospel End which had come to mean so much to her.

Rosie didn't pretend to understand the mysteries of the Methodist system, or the complexities of local church life... but she could hear the pain in Sarah's voice, all right. She also knew what it was to be hurt and rejected... and what it was to ache for another place with a pain that you couldn't describe.

'I know just how you feel,' said Rosie at last, 'when you have to leave somewhere that's so special that you think you'll never find anywhere like it again. I was in a foster home like that once. They were really nice. It was a family, see? But they didn't treat me as anything special, it was just like I was one of the kids. I lived there for over a year while my dad was in prison and me mam couldn't cope. I was so happy. It was in the country, and it was a nice house... and they were really free and easy people. They let me be me.

'But then, when me dad came out of prison and me mam got herself back together again the social workers came and took me home. I said I didn't want to go, but they had a 'conference' and decided it was for the best.

'Of course, when I got home, me mam wouldn't let me see me foster parents again. I think she was jealous; and me dad didn't want them even talked about. I wasn't even allowed to phone them an' tell them I was alright. I hated it at home after that. There was only two ways of talking in our house, threats and bribes... no-one seemed to know how to get on any other way.

'Every night I used to lie in bed and think about the foster home, and the garden, and the kids, and the toys... and I used to wish as hard as I could that one day I'd be allowed to go back and live there. But it never happened. That's why I ran away, as soon as I could, that... and other reasons.'

'What other reasons?' pried Sarah, gently.

'I can't tell you them. I can't tell anyone them.'

Now it was the turn of Sarah to cradle Rosie in her arms. She held Rosie for a long time, and as they held each other silently, the front door clicked open.

'It's only me,' said Geoff. 'I've got a surprise visitor'.

Dave entered the room grinning from ear to ear. 'I got off, bound over to keep the peace under the care and keeping of Geoff, here.'

'Well I'm damned' said Rosie, wiping tears away with her sleeve. 'I think this must be our lucky day.'

The church council meeting on Wednesday was

a strange affair from start to finish. Geoff arrived early to find the twenty-five chairs already laid out in a large circle. Ms Briggs was the only person already present, and she was sat at a small card table containing a large floral arrangement that practically hid her.

Geoff greeted her, but there was no response. Geoff registered that she looked pale and with-drawn. She was writing the date and the words 'Church Council Minutes' in a large hard-bound book. In her role as the church council secretary, she always kept a precise record of all that happened as the meeting progressed. She did not believe in taking rough notes and entering the record later.

As each person arrived Geoff greeted them with a firm handshake, and a pat on the elbow or back. The morning people sat on one side of the circle, and the evening on the other. They reminded Geoff of boxers entering a contest from different sides of the ring. He wondered if he was cast in the role of referee.

Geoff sat and watched them. How different they were! The morning congregation were into loud welcomes and long embraces. Several of the women kissed each other. Frequently they greeted one another with loud expressions of 'hallelujah' and 'praise the Lord'.

The evening congregation was much quieter in approach. They respected each other's space, and there seemed to be little or no physical contact between them, not even a handshake. This group obviously took itself very seriously.

Geoff's lectures in group dynamics at college had

taught him to observe such things. He recognised that he was not only dealing with two strands of theology, he was dealing with two different cultures and two different kinds of people.

Geoff opened the meeting with a contemporary hymn called 'Servant King'. He watched as several of the morning congregation raised their arms in worship, whilst some of the evening congregation looked awkward and refused to sing. In his opening prayer Geoff sensed that every word was being weighed and measured by the different groups present. They were trying to place him in the wide spectrum of theological opinion.

The first matters of business passed through without comment, but the atmosphere changed instantly when he naively announced the fourth item. 'Now we come to our next point on the agenda' said Geoff. 'It's the Evangelistic Mission'.

The black man with the moustache whom Geoff had noticed on Sunday morning stood up, tall and erect, and thumbed the large leather Bible in his right hand.

'Mr Chairman, this proposal is very important. We have been waiting for a decision on this matter for over eighteen months, since before the last minister left, and I don't feel that we can wait a moment longer'.

There was a chorus of 'hear, hear!'s and 'Amen's from the members of the circle to Geoff's right. Those on the left looked disturbed and uncomfortable.

Peter leant forward, his mop of hair completely covering his eyes. 'I must say that I have deep reservations about this proposal. An evangelistic mission in an area like this and at a time like this is just asking for trouble. I fear that it will do nothing but harm. It says all that's worst about the church... triumphalism, bigotry, invasion of space, and—worst of all—it will set back relationships with those of other faiths for years or even decades. Remember, we have to live in this community.'

'That's not right' said the smartly dressed businessman in the dark suit, who was again seated close to his attractive wife. 'Jesus commissioned us to go into all the world to preach the gospel, and it's about time that this church got obedient.'

Geoff interposed, 'Excuse my ignorance, but what form of mission did you have in mind? Have you been looking for an evangelist, for instance?'

Ms Briggs flicked back the pages of the large 'minute book' in front of her. 'Point of information, Mr Chairman, we have been considering an invitation to the 'Rainbow Arch Ministry Team and Healing Confederation'. It's an interdenominational and international ministry who are headed up by an American called Doctor Arthur Nodder.'

The tall black man stood again, 'Doctor Nodder has a remarkable ministry, particularly in parts of South America where his preaching is heard by tens of thousands of people each week on his radio broadcast. He comes to London every year in June because he is a tennis enthusiast, and is available for ministry either before or after the Wimbledon championships.'

The girl with long blonde hair, who on this occasion was sporting a prominent 'Greenpeace' badge, rocked back in her chair and half raised her hand to catch Geoff's attention. He nodded.

'Well, Chair, I don't have any problem with this mission as long as I don't have to have anything to do with it. As long as the money is raised by members who vote in favour, and as long as they support the meetings... who cares?'

'But surely,' Geoff pleaded, 'that's hardly the right spirit in which to embark on mission together. We should be joining in prayer, training and planning as a whole church... not just half of us!'

The man in the dark suit and the thick tinted spectacles who had spoken about French ecology on Sunday evening was growing redder by the minute. His feelings on the mission didn't bear repeating, but he was determined to repeat them, anyway.

'If by that, Mr Notes, you are suggesting that this half of the church get involved with some lunatic neo-Nazi South American evangelistic group in order to 'convert' Redbrook, you are much mistaken. The naivety of faith which some of the people here present hold is an embarrassment to many of us, and this mission will simply make the church a laughing stock.'

The tall black man with the leatherbound Bible stood up again, and rose to his full height. He looked sternly at his bespectacled opponent.

'Rather we had a naivety of faith than no faith at all, eh? I've stuck it here for these last eighteen months in the hope that something might change, but it seems to me that there's a group here who are determined to kill off the spiritual life of this church. If things don't change under Mr Notes' leadership then a good number of us will be moving on.'

There was a soft chorus of 'Amen's, and a stern cough from Ms Briggs, who was beginning to feel most uncomfortable. Peter leant forward even further than normal, and ran his hands through his hair. It was a pose of utter despair.

'Out beyond these walls is a world torn apart by racism, ageism, sexism, and er... vandalism. Yet our morning congregation has turned its back on this desperate need and is besotted with the 'bless-me mentality' which looks for emotional highs and doesn't give a damn about the needs of the...'

The immaculately dressed woman whose husband had spoken earlier was on her feet and speaking—without permission from the chair.

'Rubbish, absolute rubbish. Of course we care about the world. Just because we don't use *Socialist Worker* jargon, or talk endlessly about these things doesn't mean that we're not informed or that we don't care. Many of us happen to believe in the power of Evil, and much of what you put down to 'political mismanagement' we recognise as the work of Satan and all his demons.'

'I rest my case,' interjected Pete. 'If we go out into Redbrook and blame the problems the people here are facing on Satan and his minions we'll lose what little credibility we have. They only have to attend a borough council meeting to realise that many of their problems have an earthly origin.' He turned and addressed the previous speaker directly. 'Are you seriously suggesting that we accuse the council of demonic possession? God knows, I wouldn't trust them any further than I could throw them, but even I don't think they are evil, they're just ignorant and need educating.'

The woman turned red with anger. Her father

was a prominent local councillor. 'Don't twist my words, you know I don't mean that.'

Geoff felt this meeting was rapidly getting out of hand. He scanned the gathering for someone who might have something that wasn't inflammatory to say. His eyes came to rest on the old man he had guessed to be blind when he had seen him at the morning service on Sunday. His theory was confirmed by the presence of a Labrador lying at the man's feet. The dog wore a yellow reflective harness, and appeared to be asleep. Geoff caught Sarah's eye and nodded towards the man. 'Bert,' Sarah mouthed back at him.

'I wonder if we could hear from Bert?' He prayed that Bert wasn't an extremist of any kind.

The old man Bert got to his feet. His dog was instantly awake and attentive but didn't move.

'Believe me, friends, I want this mission more than anyone. I've longed for it... and prayed for it... for years and years. I really think that this area needs to know what we stand for and what we believe. But Geoff's right. This church is a disgrace. What's the point of bringing people to the Lord and then introducing them to a divided church. What a terrible witness! Before we can speak to the world we need to sort ourselves out.'

'Well spoken, Bert!' chimed Ms Briggs from her camouflaged position behind the flowers. 'We're all responsible adults, and we all say that we follow the same Master. Isn't it time we began to discover if there's some common ground between us?'

Sarah felt rather awkward about speaking out at this particular point in time, but she felt so angry that if she didn't say something she thought she might explode!

'Geoff and I have only been here a few days, and already we've got a couple of local people sleeping in our house because they've got nowhere to go. We're all sat here arguing about the finer points of theology while there are thousands of hurting people, all around us here in Redbrook. Can't we DO something instead of just talk? If the 'Rainbow Arch Group' is a bit divisive, isn't there something in mission that we could all agree upon?'

At that moment, when the meeting was poised for re-direction, Miriam stood up, her eyes flashing with anger. For a long time she just looked around the group, breathing heavily, and pointing at them all as she turned.

'I've been coming here for three years. Three years. And in all that time I never asked any of you for help. Three years I've attended the services, been to the fellowships, sat through the committees, paid my collection and given my support. And never did I ask for anything. Not until this week. And this week I asked you to pray for my Ben, and Geoff got the message round to meet us here at seven o'clock Monday morning. Geoff and me sat here and waited for you, didn't we Geoff? Waited until you came to join us. And out of all of you only one could spare a few minutes to come and pray for my Ben, and that was Bert. Thank you, Bert, thank you that at least you cared enough to come. So, while you're arguing about who's right and who's wrong I ask you this question. Do you believe that God can heal my Ben? And will you be here tomorrow morning? 'Cos if you don't come I think I'll have to go somewhere else for my help.'

The atmosphere was electric. Both groups sat and stared at each other and there was an uneasy silence. It was as if Miriam had cut the falsehood of their division with the sharp knife of reality. She stood for some seconds, still breathing heavily and still pointing her finger as she glared around the group.

The stillness was broken by the sound of running feet above. The tall black man leapt to his feet and raced out of the room. 'Damn kids, they'll break their stupid necks'.

'Don't worry, Mr Notes,' Ms Briggs whispered from behind her flowers, 'it happens quite often… kids on the roof. Sometimes there are so many of them up there that we wonder if they'll come through. It can be most disturbing.'

Geoff rose to his feet trying to think of something poignant to say, but words escaped him. 'Normally I like to say the benediction after church meetings, but I'd consider it blasphemy to ask God's blessing on such a meeting as this.' With that, he strode out of the room without even as much as a glance behind him.

Sarah flushed with embarrassment. It was a long time since she'd seen Geoff look so angry and stern, so she felt that her role might best be to stay behind and pour oil on troubled waters. She thanked Miriam for her challenge, and assured her that she'd be there the next morning. She shook hands with Peter, and jokingly asked if he thought the Yin and Yang had been out of sorts this evening. She embraced old Bert, and told him that he was lovely;

and ended up by helping Ms Briggs stack up the chairs.

The people were quickly gone, and only Ms Briggs and Sarah were left to put out the lights and trudge out into the bitterly cold January night. 'Why do you stick at it, Ms Briggs? Why do you stay?'

'I don't know really, Sarah. I suppose I'm hanging on in the hope of a revival. I'd hate to miss it, especially after all these years!' She smiled a shy smile. She quite liked Sarah Notes.

'Why don't you come home for supper? You can help me put Geoff back together again!'

Ms Briggs felt embarrassed. 'Well, I'd love to my dear, but I must get to bed. I do have work in the...' Her voice trailed to nothing. How stupid, there was no work in the morning. Not tomorrow. Not ever. 'Oh, all right then, if you don't mind... thank you.'

Chapter Five

Ms Briggs and Sarah were chatting happily together by the time they reached the manse. Sarah turned the key in the lock and Ms Briggs followed her in. There was the unmistakable sound of weeping coming from the lounge.

Sarah opened the lounge door and looked in disbelief at what she saw. Rosie was sitting in the armchair, her lip bleeding and her eye red with bruises. Geoff was kneeling awkwardly beside her trying to administer first aid with damp cotton wool and antiseptic.

'It's Dave,' wailed Rosie, 'he's gone... and he says he's never coming back'.

Ms Briggs quietly made her way to the kitchen to brew tea. 'Oh I am sorry, Rosie, you seemed so happy together when we left. How come it all fell apart so quickly?'

Rosie sobbed loudly, then drew a deep breath. 'We had a row about the baby. He wants me to get rid of it. There ain't no way I'm going to do that. He said he knew the truth.'

'Knew the truth about what, Rosie?', Sarah knelt on the other side of her, and placed her hand on Rosie's hand.

'He says the baby isn't his, it's someone else's, and he ain't going to be saddled with raising someone else's kid. But it is his, I swear on my life, it's his. He said he wanted to marry me, but not if I kept the baby.'

Ms Briggs entered with cups of tea. She despised mugs, and had found a few china cups at the back of the kitchen cupboard. 'Here you are, a nice cup of tea. That'll calm everyone down.'

She gently handed the tea to the three of them and stood by the door, just for a moment, and looked at them. They were all too engrossed to notice as she gently closed the lounge door behind her and went back outside into the darkness.

As she walked slowly down the busy road the picture of Geoff, Sarah and Rosie—bound together in that moment of crisis—looked to her like a magnificent sculpture or stained glass window. There was something pure and holy about it... like a glimpse of another world. How small her problems seemed, compared to Rosie's.

Gently and lovingly Sarah helped Rosie up the stairs to bed. After the scrawny girl had had a bath and was wearing one of Geoff's old shirts for nightwear, she clambered under the quilt and Sarah straightened the cover and knelt beside the bed. 'Father, thank you for Rosie, and for the new life growing inside her. We thank you Lord that when everything seems as though it's falling apart, you are still there... and still in control. Guide Rosie, that everything will work out alright. For Jesus' sake. Amen'. Rosie looked quizzically at Sarah, and then disappeared under the quilt. Sarah turned out the light and opened the door to leave, but as she did so, she turned and whispered. 'Sleep well, Rosie.'

When she got back downstairs Geoff was seated in front of the television, his eyes glazed. The moving pictures were washing over him like a therapeutic haze. He felt used by a church who wanted him to come down on one side or another in their squabble over the correct form of outreach, and especially by Dave who had cynically lied to him about his intentions to Rosie. Sarah perched herself on the sofa beside him and put an arm around his tense shoulders. She was only just seated when there was a sharp rap at the door. Sarah leapt up to answer it.

She opened the front door to find Peter standing there, his head hung low and his hair hanging over his eyes. It was as if he was embarrassed about his size. 'Hi Sarah,' he peered through the tousled hair, 'any chance of a quick word with Geoff?'

'Come in,' Sarah smiled, 'though I'm not sure if you'll get much sense out of him tonight.'

Peter entered the lounge and sprawled himself onto the empty armchair. Sarah brusquely turned off the television and disappeared into the kitchen to make some coffee. This looked like church business, and she didn't want to intrude.

Geoff was in a filthy mood, and it was clear that

Peter would have to make the first bid for conversation. He sat looking at the floor, his fingers running through his unkempt mop of hair.

'I came about tonight, Geoff. I felt you were wrong to say what you did. You had no right to deny us the benediction.'

Geoffrey Notes looked straight at Peter. 'The Church is the Body of Christ, we are ONE body... and we all belong together. Tonight the people of Redbrook were tearing it apart, limb from limb.'

'Well, I saw it as rather a creative evening, actually Geoff. I accept that there was a sharp dichotomy of opinion... but can't that be a healthy sign? We're alive? We're kicking?'

'But Peter, there was no love. That's what hurt me most.'

Peter brushed back his hair. 'I still feel you were wrong.'

Geoff smiled. 'Very well, I'm afraid we'll just have to agree to disagree.'

'Anyway, that wasn't the only reason for coming. I wondered if you needed any help with these people you mentioned. Jill and I have got quite a big place if you need some room.'

A spark of hope returned to Geoff's eyes. 'Are you serious about helping? I need to find one of them. Would you come with me, now?' Peter nodded enthusiastically.

A few minutes later Geoff climbed into Peter's large grey Saab, and the two drove off toward the centre of London at speed. 'It's this wretched government's fault, all this homelessness. They've simply emptied the mentally disturbed, the unemployed and the kids without solid homes out onto the streets.' Peter never missed an opportunity to score political points.

'No, Peter, it's our fault,' Geoff whispered, 'you and me... and everyone like us. It's just that we don't care enough. Not enough to get our hands dirty.'

The two men drove in silence to Waterloo. The last patrons of the Arts at the South Bank complex were driving away, and there was plenty of space to park. Peter locked the car and set the alarm, he'd heard a lot about Waterloo at night.

The two well dressed men descended the flight of stone stairs and paused at the bottom to gaze at the scene before them. It was so cold that their breath hung in clouds before them and the light drizzle they had driven through was turning to sleet. The long dark underpass ahead of them was lined on either side with cardboard boxes and sleeping figures. Here and there several people were huddled around small fires. The air was strong with the smell of humanity.

Peter and Geoff moved slowly up the aisle between the rows of homeless people and peered at the faces. Many were already asleep, but others sat looking silently at them with disdain in their eyes. Several older men were drinking meths around a fire. They cursed the well-dressed visitors as they passed. A teenage girl peeked out of a cardboard box and begged for money, but Geoff declined. He felt very vulnerable.

At long last they reached the end of the line. 'It's futile, Geoff, I don't think you've a chance of finding him here.' But still they turned and ambled back up the line again, peering into the boxes and searching the sleeping faces as they went. There was no sign of Dave.

They walked back to the Saab and clicked the doors unlocked. 'My God, Geoff, I'd seen it on television; but it's different being here. What the hell can we do?'

Geoff turned and looked at Peter, who was gripping the steering wheel and gazing thoughtfully out of the windscreen. 'We can begin by doing something... anything... no matter how small...'

Peter nodded silently in agreement. Something had happened in the relationship between Geoff and Peter that night. They had been bound together in the horror of a situation which would ultimately affect the course of their lives.

The following morning was bitterly cold and foggy as Geoff and Sarah ambled hand-in-hand towards the church. The sleet that had fallen the previous night now formed a thin sheet of ice that made walking hazardous. It was 6:30 am, and they'd decided to get to church early to put the heating on and to make some coffee for those who might come to pray.

Bert, accompanied by his guide dog, arrived first at 6:45 am, and sat quietly in a corner. As usual he was smiling, his face wrinkled but radiant. He was very appreciative of the cup of coffee.

Then came Ms Briggs, carrying a large handbag and an umbrella. She went to the kitchen to help Sarah make the coffee. 'What an awful morning!'

'Yes, I bet you're dreading that journey up to town' said Sarah, unaware of Ms Briggs' change of circumstances.

'Well actually,' she smiled, 'I've not got to go to work today.'

Adam, the tall black man with the leatherbound Bible, had brought his wife and three children along. They were immaculately dressed, as always, and the twins had pink ribbons in their hair. Adam's son, Daniel, looked vaguely familiar to Geoff. The young teenager looked distinctly uncomfortable, and Geoff could only guess at the family negotiations that had occurred to get him there.

Peter looked decidedly embarrassed. Prayer meetings weren't his thing. He had come as an expression of solidarity rather than to take part.

There was an awkwardness among them as the morning people and the evening people of Redbrook church gathered together for their first joint prayer meeting. Miriam stood silently sipping her coffee. Her eyes were red, and the dark shadows under them revealed something of the strain she was under.

At ten past seven Geoff drew the thirty members to order. They were seated in a circle. 'This morning we're going to pray for Ben, and I'm going to ask each of you to think of an aspect of this situation and bring it to God.'

Geoff listed a number of possibilities. The doctors, the nurses, the consultant. He suggested they pray for Ben, for Miriam, and for the hospital in general. 'Please feel free to pray as you wish, and I'll close at the end,' suggested Geoff hesitantly.

They bowed their heads in solemn silence, and a heavy cloud of embarrassment filled the air. The silence continued, all except for the hum of the fan in the large gas heater at the back of church. Geoff longed for someone to say something and surreptitiously lifted his shirt cuff. It was 7:15. Five minutes... and no-one had prayed. Geoff was getting decidedly uncomfortable, why was no-one praying?

It was 7:20 before Bert stood and spoke to the Lord. Geoff breathed a long sigh of relief. 'Lord Jesus, you are here with us this morning, and that's all that matters. You are the one who loves us, you are the one who walks beside us, you are the one who never leaves us nor forsakes us... and we love you, Lord.'

There was a chorus of Amens. Geoff felt irritated, why hadn't Bert even mentioned Ben? This prayer meeting was a disaster. After several more moments of awkward silence Geoff finished the meeting. He prayed a long and detailed prayer listing aspects of the situation, rather like a shopping list of needs for God to meet.

As people got up to go Miriam stood in her prophetic pose... finger pointing. 'Firstly, I want to say thank you all for coming and I hope you'll all be here tomorrow.' It was not so much an invitation, as a command. There was no 'secondly'.

Sarah interposed, 'Miriam, we're all right behind you? Is there anything we can do to help?'

There were nods of agreement from around the circle. 'Yes, there is just one thing. The consultant thinks that Ben may be able to hear but not to respond. He asked if anyone whose voice Ben might know would be willing to come and talk to him... it might...' Miriam sat down, and fought to compose herself.

'Of course, of course' said Geoff, softly. 'Is there anyone here who may be able to help?'

Pip, the girl with the long blonde hair, who was today sporting a brightly coloured 'Save the whale' badge half-raised her hand. 'Ben's in my cub-pack, I don't mind going... if it's any help.'

The tall black man smoothed his moustache. 'I was teaching Ben in the Sunday school. I would like to see him. Is that okay Miriam.'

'Thanks, Adam,' she nodded as she wiped her eyes with a red silk handkerchief, 'maybe I'll see you both there at six o'clock this evening?'

Geoff and Sarah walked silently hand-in-hand back to the manse. Geoff was far away in his thoughts. Sarah looked up at him, this man she loved, but still didn't fully understand. She knew that prayer meetings weren't his strong point, and that this morning's had devastated him.

'How about a huge breakfast at that transport cafe in the high street?' Sarah smiled. 'There's nothing like a prayer meeting to give you an appetite!'

'You're on!' Geoff's love of junk food remained from his student days.

Geoff and Sarah sat opposite one another in the window seat of the 'Redbrook Diner' and tucked into a huge mixed grill. The walls were covered with pictures of football teams and photos of partially clad young women. Geoff and Sarah were surrounded by lorry drivers and local road repairmen, but it didn't seem to matter. Geoff smiled at Sarah, her dark hair shining in the morning light and whispered, 'This has got to be the most romantic meal we've had together in ages.'

'Almost as romantic as that night in the Bristol restaurant?'

'Bristol restaurant? Which one do you mean?' Geoff smiled innocently.

'The one when you proposed to me, stupid.'

'Oh, *that* restaurant.'

Sarah smiled warmly as she savoured the memory of that special night. She rubbed her knee against his.

'I'm glad you said yes, Sarah.'

'So am I, Geoff.'

'Pass the ketchup, mate' said a huge man in a boiler suit. Geoff dutifully passed the ketchup into the oil-stained hand. 'Thanks, mate', the man smiled and winked a knowing wink. Geoff flushed with embarrassment. The precious moment was broken.

At six o'clock that evening Miriam was seated in her normal position looking at Ben's doll-like face. Pip was seated opposite, overcome with the horror of the situation. She fiddled restlessly with her long bead necklace and tried to think of something to say.

'Ben, it's me... Pip, your Akela...' She paused, trying to imagine that he could hear. 'The boys from the pack all send you greetings. We had a good meeting on Tuesday, we were learning how to light oil lamps.'

Pip looked over at Miriam, looking for some kind of moral support, but Miriam was studying Ben's face for some flicker of movement, some vague signal of hope. Pip looked back at Ben again. The dull rhythm of the respirator continued.

'Gavin was his usual mischievous self. I had to take the matches off him, or else he might have

burnt the church down. Oh, and we played football... with the soft ball... like we usually do. The
boys in the pack want you in the team for the next
big match... if you can make it.'

The door-flap opened and Adam poked his head
round. 'May I come in?' he said in a stage whisper.
Miriam stood and beckoned him to her seat. Adam
stroked his moustache and lowered himself awkwardly past the buzz of machinery and into the
chair.

'Ben, I thought you'd like to know that your
uniform has arrived, and I've got your cap here.'
Pip took it awkwardly out of her anorak pocket and
laid it on the pillow next to him. She looked at
Adam as if giving a cue.

Adam's deep West Indian drawl was mellow and
reassuring. 'Ben, my young friend, this is Adam...
from the Sunday school. I have come to bring the
love of the other kids, especially Phyllis and Marie,
the twins. They... they all miss you... and they've
drawn you some pictures, for the wall here.' He
placed several brightly painted pictures of sea and
boats and a storm on the cabinet near the bed, and
then blew his nose very loudly into a voluminous
handkerchief.

Adam looked back at Miriam who was standing
at the foot of the bed gazing up at a monitor and
wondering what it meant. 'The pictures show the
story we were doing together. The one where Jesus
was asleep in a boat, and the boat was sinking...
but then Jesus stood up and commanded...' Adam
paused, and then shouted at the top of his voice 'BE
STILL!'

'It changed' shrieked Miriam. 'It changed...

when you shouted. The line went up and down. Nurse, nurse, come here quickly.' A young staff nurse entered almost immediately. 'Nurse', Miriam continued, 'When he shouted... the line on the screen changed. It really changed.'

The nurse smiled sympathetically. 'Yes, I'm sure it did. It does change sometimes, just for a moment, but it doesn't always mean too much. But I'll put it on the notes... the doctor would like to know.' She smiled again, and left as quickly as she had arrived.

The flap opened again, and Geoff was standing there looking serious and drawn. He placed his arm around Miriam's shoulders and squeezed her gently. He looked at Adam and Pip, frozen like statues as they stared at the motionless face and muttered, 'Thanks for coming.'

At last Adam turned to him. 'Pastor Notes, I really think it's time to use the balm of Gilead. The oil of healing.' He dug deep into his pocket and pulled out a small glass bottle containing golden oil.

Geoff took the oil and paused for a moment as he wondered what to do. He'd never prayed for healing before... not directly... not like this. Oh he'd asked God to make so-and-so better from their sore throat or what ever, but this seemed fundamentally different, this was moving into areas of spirituality that he personally had no experience of. He manoeuvred his way past the equipment until he was leaning over Pip. Miriam squeezed past and knelt in front of Adam. At Geoff's bidding the three of them touched Ben's warm hands while he unscrewed the plastic stopper and poured the oil onto the palm of his left hand. He placed the bottle gently down, and dipped his right forefinger into the holy unction.

'Gentle Jesus' he whispered, gently marking the sign of a cross on the boy's forehead 'you let the little children come to you, and so we lift Ben before you now, asking, gentle Jesus, that you would bring him up from the depths of unconsciousness to be with us again. As I anoint Ben with the sign of the cross, I invite you to pour your healing grace upon him now. Amen'. The other three whispered 'Amen', and after Miriam had gently kissed her son on the forehead, they walked silently out of the cubicle and down the busy corridors. Somewhere in the distance a bell was ringing. Visiting time had ended.

Geoff got into his car and turned the ignition. The music of a local pop station filled the vehicle, and he flicked the radio off. He felt close to God and wanted silence. In that shared moment with the oil the four of them had shared something mystic, a sense of the presence of the Lord.

As his car pulled into the terrace Geoff noticed a figure sitting on the step of number thirty-two. His heart leapt with relief. He got out and slammed the door... 'Dave, is that you?'

There was no reply, so Geoff locked up and strolled toward the house. Dave was sitting on the doorstep, cigarette in hand, and blowing a thick blue streak of smoke upwards as he gazed at the sky.

'Are you okay? We were worried.' Geoff tried to sound understanding. He was still angry at the way Dave had treated Rosie, and for the fact that he had run off while bound over into Geoff's care.

'Yep. I'm just fine,' the young man replied sarcastically. 'But I've got nowhere to sleep tonight, and your wife won't let me in here.'

'Get in the car, Dave,' Geoff smiled, 'I've got just the place for you.' In under five minutes Geoff and Dave were sat in Pete's front room drinking coffee and passing the time of day like old friends.

Pete worked for the design office of a large electronics firm. Essentially, however, he was a people person and the long hours he spent each day in front of a design board frustrated him. Although his job was intellectually challenging it had never really fulfilled him.

Pete's wife Jill entered with a plate of hot buttered currant buns. She was very attractive and had the kind of bubbly personality that lit up every room she entered. Jill dedicated her life to work in a national animal rights charity and to the care of three Siamese cats, which were the joy of her life. Pete and Jill had no children.

'How's your day been, Geoff?' Jill asked nicely, 'Been to see Miriam's kid?'

'Yes, I was there this evening. There's no change, but Pip and Adam have been talking to him.'

'What, together... I mean... both of them in the same place at the same time?' Jill interjected.

'Yes. They both did very well'. Geoff was scoffing a second currant bun: he hadn't realised how hungry he was. Jill left to get some cake.

Pete smiled. His head was resting awkwardly on his hands. 'Well, that's a miracle, for a start. Pip and Adam haven't spoken to each other since the last minister left.' He felt he'd already said too much, so he disjointedly changed the subject. He turned to Dave. 'Well, Dave,' Pete said, as he began to stroke his mop of hair, 'we've got a big place here. Feel free to stay here for a week or two... if you want.'

Dave stubbed out his cigarette in the ash-tray provided. 'Thanks. That would suit me fine.'

Chapter Six

Geoffrey Notes had a lousy night's sleep. So much was going on beneath the surface with the people at Redbrook that he wondered if he'd ever understand it. His problems at Gospel End had been bad enough, but somehow the people in Yorkshire were more straightforward and easier to understand.

What was more, he was dreading the arrival of morning. Another prayer meeting, another round in the contest between the 'morning' people and the 'evening' people, another prolonged silence.

By six o'clock Geoff had eaten a large bowl of instant porridge, drunk two cups of strong coffee... and was leaving for the church.

He sat in the cold and empty church and looked at the circle of chairs around him. He pictured each person sitting in each seat and quietly committed them to God. He prayed for a melting of the icy coldness between them, and for the unifying power of God's Spirit to bring them together as one.

Ridiculous as it seemed, he also prayed for the

prayer meeting. He couldn't face another awkward session like yesterday, and felt that if a church couldn't pray for a sick child it didn't have much credibility left. He asked for God's presence to fill the place, as He had the previous evening in the hospital.

At six-thirty the door opened and Bert shuffled in with his guide dog. 'Morning, Bert,' Geoff called out, so that the newcomer would know he was not alone.

'Morning Geoff, just the man I wanted to talk to.' Geoff helped Bert to the seat beside him, and the dog flopped to the floor and promptly fell asleep.

'There are things that you should know, Geoff. Reasons for the way things are.'

'Go on,' Geoff said, reassuringly.

'Well, no-one prayed yesterday because there's a lot of ill-feeling among us. Some of the morning people feel they can't even talk to the evening people, let alone pray with them.'

'Has it been like this a long time, Bert?' asked Geoff sympathetically.

'Well, your predecessor here was a fine young man, full of the Holy Spirit. He taught us so much about receiving God's power... and about healing, and prophecy... and all the gifts of the Holy Spirit. There were some of us who were right behind him... and we supported him all the way. But there were others who felt shut out... like they weren't good enough Christians. That's why they started meeting separately.'

'And what can I do to unravel it all?' said Geoff, despondently.

Bert paused for a long time, fiddling with the reign to his guide dog as he pondered the situation. 'I've just the one dog showing me the way. If I had two, I think I'd fall over. For the last eighteen months we've had Adam pulling one way, and Pip the other. A lot of us are caught up in the middle.'

Just then Sarah burst in with a cheery 'Morning folks,' and went to make the coffee. Geoff reached over and squeezed Bert's hand. 'God must grieve to see a church as divided as this,' and got up to help with the coffee. 'Oh, I meant to ask. Your dog, what's his name?' When Bert told him Geoff smiled. Trigger merely twitched an ear.

Very soon afterwards the others started to arrive. It was altogether peculiar, meeting so early in the morning, and everyone together. After they had all collected their coffee and sat down Geoff leant forward, and everyone took it as a cue for silence.

'I'm really grateful that you've all come back today. I felt the meeting was a bit of a disaster yesterday, and I'm really hoping it'll be different today. But I need to talk plainly, just for a few minutes. We all know that this is a divided church... the morning crowd and the evening crowd... and it's little wonder that when we come together we all feel awkward.'

Geoff paused to look around and gauge reactions. People were listening intently. 'I also recognise that we all see the faith differently, and we've all got different experiences of the Spirit. But if we can't pray together... well, the whole thing is just a sham. Worthless. While we hold our hurts and resentments little Ben is lying in that hospital... '

Geoff's lips quivered with emotion. 'Shame on us... shame on us.'

Sarah had to speak out. She knew how deeply moved Geoff was. This was no act, his heart was breaking with the pain of this divided people. 'Geoff's right, how can God bless us as a church if we continue to live such separate lives? Besides, you've all got so much to teach each other... if you could only see it.' She flushed with embarrassment, feeling she'd said far too much.

Geoff sighed. 'I know this is going to be very difficult for some of you, but I want us to hold hands together... round this circle. It's a symbol that, with all our differences, we're drawn together to support Ben... and, of course, Miriam.'

Geoff reached out a hand to Bert on one side, and to Pete on the other. Slowly and movingly the hands were linked, and the circle made complete. 'This morning, please say a prayer if you can. I felt you were all riding on my faith yesterday. I know you all like to pray in different ways, but God understands. Lots of simple one-liners would be a start, okay?'

The gathered circle gripped each other's hands tight, and together, at Geoff's suggestion they prayed the Lord's Prayer. For many of them the words seemed sharply relevant. 'OUR Father... THY will be done... FORGIVE US our trespasses... Deliver us from evil... THINE is the kingdom...'

And then the prayers flowed. Simple, short, profound. Some heavy with the language of Canaan, others cold and sharply formed petitions. But it didn't seem to matter, for here was a church crying out to God for a little boy called Ben.

By eight o'clock everyone had gone except for Sarah and Ms Briggs who were washing up the coffee cups together. Geoff had taken Miriam up to the hospital to begin her daily vigil at Ben's bedside.

'Much better today, wasn't it?' said Ms Briggs encouragingly.

'Yes, better than yesterday, anyway' sighed Sarah, 'It's so sad to see a church divided by theology.'

'Mmm, I wouldn't put it down to theology... I'd say it was something to do with experience.' Ms Briggs clutched a pile of cups and began to stack them in the cupboard. Having unloaded her fragile cargo, she continued.

'We were never that united a church, not close, I mean. But when the last minister was here something quite wonderful happened in the fellowship group that met in the manse. One night, when they were all praying together, something happened... and they changed. They really *did* change. It was as if they discovered what it's all about. But I was doing a lot of overtime in those days... and I just couldn't get to the meetings. I've no doubt that they found something very special... but the rest of us somehow got left behind. Pip was so involved with her scouting, and Pete with his politics... we all felt shut out. Pip formed us into a discussion meeting, and that's when we split the morning and evening services.'

Sarah wiped the draining board. 'How can Geoff put you all back together?'

Ms Briggs smiled. 'I think that might be a little beyond Geoff, knowing us lot.'

'But not beyond God...' Sarah muttered under her breath.

The two women locked up the church and walked up the busy road amid the roar of rush-hour traffic. 'No work again today Ms Briggs?'

'No, no work today. I've been made redundant.' The words tumbled out without emotion, but the minute she'd said them she regretted having revealed her secret. She wasn't ready to talk.

Sarah sensed the pain behind the statement and continued 'I'm so sorry. Do you want to talk?'

'No, not yet' the older woman was adamant. 'But I'll come and see you when I am... if you don't mind'.

Sarah smiled, 'Anytime.' And as they went their separate ways she called 'By the way, what's your Christian name?'

Ms Briggs paused, then turned and called 'Margaret'.

Meanwhile, in the intensive care ward at the hospital, Miriam had taken her usual seat and was looking intently at Ben's face to see if there was any noticeable change. She felt sure that God had heard the prayers of his people.

Geoff bade her farewell and strolled down the corridor. He no longer felt a stranger here, and some of the staff greeted him by name. They had grown to like this young minister with his unusually casual approach to chaplaincy.

Geoff stood silently in the large lift as it descended the four floors. Finally, a bell sounded.

They had reached the ground level. As the doors of the lift opened they revealed the dark suited consultant standing with a younger doctor in a white coat. 'Ah, you're the minister I met the other day, aren't you... any chance of a chat?'

The senior doctor took him by the arm and led him into a room filled with locked glass-fronted cupboards containing medicine bottles of every shape and size. 'I think this is about as private a place as we'll find this morning. I wanted to thank you for your support in this tragic case with young Ben Robins.'

Geoff nodded in appreciation, 'Thanks, it's not been easy...'

The doctor interjected, 'But I must warn you, it's looking pretty bleak and hopeless. We've just got the results from the brain scan, and they don't give us much cause for hope. I think we should start to prepare Mrs Robins for the worst.'

'There's no hope at all?' Geoff asked, pleadingly.

'Not realistically, no. I think the most humane thing we can do is to turn the respirator off. He would die quite quickly, probably in an hour or even less.'

'Isn't there anything else? No other option?'

'We've talked about transferring him to the special neurosurgical unit in the centre of London; but I doubt if he'd survive the journey. Even if he did, I'm not really convinced that they could do anything more there than we're doing here, Mr Notes,' the consultant said gravely. 'You must believe me when I say we've tried everything. Ben's head injuries are beyond healing, and even if he woke this moment he would be severely brain damaged. In my opinion, and in the opinion of several of my eminent colleagues, he will never regain consciousness.'

'So who decides when to...?' Geoff couldn't bring himself to say 'pull the plug'.

In this situation, Mr Notes, I think that one of the most qualified is yourself. Tell us when you feel Mrs Robins is prepared, and we'll take it from there.'

'Thanks, doctor' Geoff muttered, thinking 'thanks for nothing.' The interview was over and Geoff made his way back to his car. He was deep in thought.

He didn't want to talk to anyone, and felt he needed space to be alone with God. He parked next to one of the large Redbrook tower blocks and ambled past the tall building towards the recreation ground. It was bitterly cold, and a chill wind gusted around the building. He shivered.

Redbrook recreation ground bore all the marks of an inner city area. The walls were covered with colourful graffiti, and the windows of the gardener's hut were smashed and boarded up. The scraps of paper which littered the grass were being shunted this way and that by the prevailing wind.

Geoff pulled up the collar of his bright blue ski jacket and sank his hands deep into the warm pockets as he walked. He felt tense and depressed. He'd never really reckoned on the possibility that Ben might die, and the dark prospect of such an event filled him with a sickly dread.

How could he prepare Miriam for the worst when the whole church was praying for Ben's recovery. And where was God in all this? Surely

God didn't want Ben to die, not like this... not without even waking up, just once.

Geoff walked around the small recreation ground several times, then mounted the cold stone staircase of the tower block, floor upon floor, level upon level... until at last he arrived breathlessly on the twelfth floor.

He stood on the open verandah and looked out over Redbrook. The chill grey morning made the place look even bleaker than usual. He gazed down at the recreation ground and the other towering flats beyond; and across at the rows of terraced houses, and the manse. He watched the slowly moving line of morning traffic, the snaking silver tube train, and overhead the slow progression of aircraft bound for Heathrow. From here he could see the Telecom tower in the distance and the heart of the nation's capital. Millions of people lived in this vast city with its extremes of unimaginable wealth and power and utter poverty and helplessness. He stood motionless and watched the ceaseless hum of city life.

He had only been at Redbrook for ten days, yet already his life was so interwoven with the needs of its people. A dying boy, a divided church, a pregnant girl, a violent young man. He felt helpless, and powerless to help people with such enormous needs. He couldn't hack it. He didn't feel up to the job.

As he stood in the biting wind he looked down again at the recreation ground and saw the unmistakable figure of Adam strolling across towards the flats. On impulse he turned to the lift and made his way to the ground floor just as Adam was approaching the main entrance.

'Pastor Notes... good to see you. You look very cold. Why not come up to my place for some coffee?'

Geoff gave the man a wan smile and agreed, and a few minutes later he was stood in the living room beside an old paraffin heater warming his hands. Adam was preparing coffee and continuing to talk, his booming voice resounding from the kitchen.

'I'm so pleased you've come to see me. I was hoping for some fellowship, pastor. Enid, my wife, she's working up the hospital... but I'm between jobs at the moment. Things are a bit difficult in the work situation as you know.'

Adam entered the ornately decorated lounge carrying a tray. On it was a beautifully embroidered lace cover, two china cups and saucers, and a silver plate filled with chocolate biscuits. Geoff and Adam both sat on the settee together.

'How are you settling in, Pastor? These first few days can't have been easy.'

Geoff forced a smile, even though his whole being felt like a huge lump of lead. 'No, they haven't been easy, Adam.' He bit into a chocolate digestive.

'And how is the good Lord blessing you?' Adam asked with a huge smile, his eyes glinting in the dim room. 'Has the Lord given you a vision about Redbrook, Pastor?'

Geoff felt embarrassed. He had never endured such direct questioning about his spiritual life; and today of all days he didn't want to discuss it. His mind raced for a way of diverting the conversation. 'It's cold today.' But Adam wasn't listening.

'The Lord told me that you'd be coming here today, and I saw a picture of a man weighed down by bags. He had cases and carrier bags and a haversack, and he was completely bowed down by them.' Adam looked Geoff directly in the eye. 'And Pastor, I saw that the man was you.'

Geoff took another bite from his chocolate biscuit, and felt not only embarrassed but a little angry. How dare this church member make such statements about his Minister? Yet, with things so delicately balanced at the church, he certainly didn't want to alienate the man. 'Do you think it'll snow?'

Adam put down his coffee cup and biscuit to allow his hands free expression as he spoke. 'You see, Pastor Notes, the good Lord told me that he was sending you to my house for a little bit of ministry.'

'Ministry?' Geoff Notes looked decidedly uncomfortable. Why couldn't the man just talk about the weather like any other new acquaintance?

'Yes, Geoffrey. You need to lay down these many heavy weights that you are carrying around and receive the fresh empowering of God's Holy Spirit. For the good Lord promised, in John's gospel Chapter 14, that He would send us a Helper, a Counsellor... a Comforter. You need that Helper for your work in Redbrook, Geoffrey.'

Geoff Notes had never wanted to run away from a situation so much in his life. He longed to be out of this dimly lit room and away from this tall man who was waving his hands around and smiling with glee. But something, Geoff didn't know what, kept him rooted to the spot.

Before Geoff could summon up the nerve to protest, Adam had taken the cup out of his hand, moved the plastic coffee table, and asked his Pastor to kneel on the hearth rug. Geoffrey Notes did as he was told, though if he could have seen an alternative he would have taken it.

Adam placed his large black hands on Geoff's head and began to pray the most beautiful prayer Geoff had ever heard. It was a prayer of adoration and worship to King Jesus, and it was delivered with great passion in Adam's unmistakable West Indian drawl. Geoff was shocked and alarmed as Adam described his leaden feeling to the Lord, and commanded that he be set free of the weights which were dragging him down.

The experience was sudden and electric. Geoff felt that every nerve and sinew of his body was on fire, and he was shaking with an energy which was plainly not his own. His head filled with a blazing white light which burned into the deep recesses of his mind. His heart was racing and his whole being seemed to burst with joy. Geoff found himself laughing uncontrollably, and a sense of the warm embrace of God wrapped him round.

'Hallelujah' Adam shouted, 'Praise the Lord!' Somewhere in the depths of his being Geoff wondered if the neighbours could hear. Then, almost as quickly as it had come, the overwhelming sense of God went again. But Geoff was different and he stood up feeling like everything was under control. God could be trusted. All things were working together for good, after all.

'Now Geoffrey', Adam beamed, 'I think you need another cup of coffee. But this time... a strong one... yes?'

'Yes, as strong as possible.' Geoff stood at the

window and lifted the heavy net curtain. He looked out over Redbrook again. The cold chill morning remained, but Geoff knew that his perspective had changed.

Adam re-entered the room with the second tray of coffee. 'And how is young Ben today? Have you heard?'

Geoff sat down again, 'The news isn't good Adam. Can you keep a confidence?'

'Yes, Pastor, with my life.'

'The consultant thinks we should turn the respirator off. He wants me to prepare Miriam, and tell him when the time is right.'

Adam whispered a solemn 'Glory'.

'What do you think?' Geoff searched Adam's face and watched him solemnly stroke his moustache.

'What do I think? I think that the good Lord knows best, that's what I think. We will pray... but if the Lord wants to take young Ben, then we must let him go. When they turn the respirator off we will all stand together and pray... and wait upon the good guidance of our precious Lord Jesus.' Geoff marvelled at the naive simplicity of the other man's faith.

Over at Pete and Jill Bramwell's place, Dave, their new lodger, was having a great time. Pete had told him to make himself at home before he had left for work, and Jill had shown him how to adjust the central heating before she had headed off to the charity shop where she was overseeing a refit. With the house empty, he could really treat it like his own. The stereo stack was tuned in to a local pop station and the whole house filled with the regular thud of the rhythm. Dave was lying up to his neck in a foam-filled, apricot-scented bath, a bottle of Pete's treasured twelve year old malt whisky in his right hand and a cigarette in his left. He was trying to work out what to do.

He couldn't believe that this hospitality could last long, it was just too good to be true. The more he thought of Rosie, the more convinced he was that he didn't want the hassle of looking after a kid. If anything should go wrong Geoff would certainly take him back to the police, and he'd be in a worse state than ever. His best chance was to get a lot of money, and to get as far away as he could... and quickly.

The more he lay and thought, and the more that he drank, the more that Dave hated Pete and Jill and all they stood for. If he had had their advantages in life he wouldn't be in the mess he was in now, homeless and without a job. How could they understand his needs, with their two cars, four bedroom suburban house and all mod cons? How dare they salve their middle class consciences at his expense. Who the hell did they think they were? They had no idea what it was like to suffer the way he had. A sense of jealousy and hatred rose within him. He wanted to hurt them, and to make them understand what it was like to suffer. It would make them better people. Dave smiled, but there was no warmth in it.

He began off in the master bedroom and worked methodically through the house. This was not a new experience for him. He knew the secret places people liked to hide things, the places they thought were safe. He carefully searched every nook and cranny for money and jewellery. He didn't want anything big, it would be too difficult to carry and too risky to sell quickly. In various hiding places around the house he dug out two hundred pounds and several precious rings and necklaces.

Next, he finished off the last dregs of the bottle of whisky, and set about making a statement about Pete and Jill's smug suburban lifestyle. He turned each room upside down, scattering the contents of each drawer and cupboard, and smashing anything that seemed of any value. He really enjoyed smashing the picture frames which contained smiling pictures of Pete and Jill, the perfect happy couple. And the more he destroyed, the more damage he wanted to do. His actions had become frenzied, almost out of control. It was then that he saw one of Jill's cats, purring contentedly on the settee. It seemed to epitomise all that he hated in this middle class world.

The cat looked up at him with mild curiosity, its blue Siamese eyes serenely observing his actions. It seemed to regard him with the same detached interest as Dave's first social worker. Dave struggled to focus on the cat, his vision blurred by the whisky, and a powerful rage rose within him like an ocean wave. He stopped his frenzied destruction and approached the animal. It looked back at him for a moment and then closed it's eyes and curled up. The blow on the head with the empty whisky bottle was strong and swift and the poor animal died instantly. The blood from the gaping wound seeped slowly out onto the settee and dripped to the carpet below.

Dave stood over the settee for a few moments and

gazed down at the dead cat. His rage ebbed away and he suddenly felt queasy. Breathing deeply and avoiding looking at the settee Dave snatched up his spoils, buttoned his coat, and crept quietly out of the back door. He was bound for Victoria Coach station, and the bus for Birmingham.

Chapter Seven

Sarah returned from the prayer meeting to continue work on the house. She draped dust-sheets over the furniture in the back bedroom, and was stirring the paint when she became aware of Rosie standing in the doorway.

'Need any help?' Rosie puffed at her cigarette.

'If you don't mind. I've got a spare tray and roller. Thanks!'

The two women worked hard throughout the morning, chatting as they painted about anything and everything. Sarah got off the ladder, and poured more paint into her tray.

'What about the baby? How many months are you?'

'Four,' Rosie retorted, splattering the wall with wet paint, 'and no, I never considered an abortion. I always thought that Dave and me would get things together.'

'Do you love Dave?' Sarah turned and studied Rosie's face.

Rosie smiled a big smile. 'What is this... are you some kind of agony aunt or something?'

'No, just curious.'

'I miss him, if that's what you mean. Even after what he did to me. He gets in these moods, see? Then he doesn't know what he's doing.' Rosie's black eye was still clearly visible.

'Why don't I phone him over at Pete and Jill's place and arrange a meeting?' Sarah wasn't sure how good an idea this was, but if Dave was the baby's father then he ought to be encouraged to take some responsibility for it, even if that amounted to only a few pounds of maintenance once the child was born.

'Maybe,' Rosie sighed, 'but I really don't think he's interested.'

It was after four o'clock in the afternoon when Jill returned from her voluntary work at the animal rights charity shop. She turned the key in the front door and called inside, 'Hi, Dave... how's your day been?' There was no reply, perhaps he had popped out. She made her way to the kitchen to brew some tea, and stood in the doorway horrified by what she saw. Cups, saucers and plates had been swept out of the cupboards and were lying, cracked and broken, all over the floor.

As if in a daze she walked from room to room and peeked in through each door. The place was ransacked. Clothes were strewn everywhere, picture frames smashed, and chairs upturned. Jill was shivering with emotion by the time she picked up the bedside phone. 'Pete, the house has been vandalised... come home, please.' Her voice was quaking so she put down the phone and sat on the bed. She stared in disbelief at the chaos around her.

In less than five minutes the doorbell rang. It was Sarah Notes, flushed and breathless. 'Pete rang and told me to come... he'll be back as soon as he can get through the traffic.' She looked into the kitchen. 'Oh my God, what a mess... Jill, I am sorry. You sit down and I'll bring you a strong cup of tea. I hope you don't mind, I've left a note asking Geoff to come round as soon as he gets home.' Jill nodded and walked slowly towards the living room.

Sarah was just plugging in the kettle when she heard Jill's scream of despair. She ran in to find her holding the dead cat and rocking it gently in her arms. Sarah managed to persuade Jill to sit down and then she gently lifted the cat out of her arms. She took it outside into the garden. A few minutes later she was back in the lounge with a strong cup of sweet tea.

'Those cats, they're like children to me,' Jill whispered, staring into space, 'stupid really, but they're all so different... special... irreplaceable.'

'Have you called the police?' Sarah asked, hoping to change the subject.

'No,' Jill replied softly, still staring, 'we mustn't call the police. Please don't do that.'

'Why not? I'm sure you should,' Sarah insisted, firmly.

'Because Dave did it, and if he's caught he'll definitely go to prison.'

At that moment Sarah heard a key turning in the lock. Pete had made it through the rush-hour crawl and he strode confidently into the house to take control of things. He was totally unprepared for what he found and his face drained of colour when he saw the blood on his wife's clothes. 'Have the police been yet?' he asked faintly, after he had been reassured that the red stain was not human blood. 'I called them from the office.'

Jill stood up and went to him. 'We can't involve the police, darling. We don't know what happened or why he did it. We don't even know for certain that it was Dave.'

Peter stared at her. 'Of course it was Dave, who else do you think it was? He has to be found and punished. Look at what he's done.'

But Jill was adamant, 'No, Peter, you said when you got involved with Dave that you were willing to pay the price of caring... well, this is it. So for God's sake don't whinge now.'

The door-bell rang, and Pete stood looking at his wife in disbelief. 'That'll be the police, what do you suggest we say? I'm sorry to have bothered you constable... please go away.' He sounded very sarcastic.

Jill pushed him to one side, snatched a coat from the peg and wrapped it round her. She swung round to face her husband. 'Look, Peter, I will not be responsible for sending Dave to prison... not until I've discovered why he did this to us.' She was immovable in her conviction.

Jill opened the door to reveal two uniformed officers, one male and the other female. 'Hello there,' Jill smiled, 'thanks so much for coming... but there's been a dreadful mistake. I really thought the house had been burgled, but it was just the lodger. There's nothing to worry about... everything's under control. I'm dreadfully sorry for having bothered you.'

The policewoman looked at her colleague suspiciously, but he shrugged his shoulders and turned to go. 'Very well then Ma'am,' she sighed, 'but do call us again if you need to.'

Jill closed the front door. 'Now, where shall we begin?' she asked. 'I'm going to change... and then let's start upstairs and clear up one room at a time. Can you give us a hand, Sarah, just for a few minutes?'

'I'm here until it's all done,' Sarah announced, equally firmly.

Peter knew that when Jill was in a mood like this it was a waste of time to argue. He would simply have to go along with her wishes. 'After all,' he reasoned, 'she's had enough knocks for one day.'

The three of them began in the master bedroom, and they soon realised what a painstakingly slow job it was going to be. The splinters of glass from broken frames and mirrors had scattered everywhere, and the more they swept the more fragments of glass seemed to appear.

Geoff arrived after about an hour. He was still riding high after his experience of the Spirit, and wasn't really prepared for the scene of devastation which greeted him. He blanched white when he entered the ransacked lounge, and asked if anyone had been injured when he saw the blood covering the settee.

The two women nominated Geoff and Pete to go and bury the cat at the bottom of the back garden before it was too dark. They looked a strange sight,

Pete carrying a shovel, and Geoff carrying the cat—
which he had found in the garden where Sarah had
left it. Geoff had neatly wrapped it in a blue plastic
bin liner.

The two men took it in turns to dig. They
decided on a deep grave, in case the cat's bones
should be uncovered at a later date and cause Jill
more distress.

'We must have been stark raving mad to have
had that homeless lunatic living in our home,' Pete
moaned, his long mop of hair bouncing as he dug,
'and you should have warned us what we were
taking on, Geoff.'

'I'm sorry Pete, I'd no idea he'd be so stupid.'

Pete rammed the shovel into the earth, as if in
anger. 'I think we should have called the police and
shopped him. There's no way that lunatics like him
should be allowed to roam the streets.'

'Why did he do it?' Geoff asked, trying to be
helpful.

'How the hell should I know? He must be an
imbecile,' Peter added, tossing earth off the spade.

'Either that... or a cry for help.'

'A cry for help? By wrecking my house and kill-
ing my cat? We were willing to listen to him... all
he had to do was talk.' Breathless, he handed the
spade to Geoff. 'Don't give me that pseudo-psycho-
logical garbage. He's a nutter.'

'Do you love Dave, then?' Geoff paused, and
leant on the spade as he looked into Pete's face
through the dim twilight.

'No. I hate the bastard.'

'I wonder how many other people feel the same
way about him. In the few days I've known him

he's been involved in a public brawl, assaulted his pregnant girlfriend, devastated the home of two people who were trying to help him and murdered their cat. I wouldn't be surprised if the whole world hates Dave Wilson.' Geoff continued digging.

'It wouldn't surprise me in the least.' Pete pushed his mop of hair away. 'You can certainly add me to the list.'

'Then maybe you've got more of a problem than Dave.' Geoff paused from shifting the heavy soil and looked directly at Pete. 'Love your enemies, Peter.'

'It wasn't your home he flaming well wrecked.' Pete turned on his heels and walked briskly toward the house. Geoff continued to dig. The door of the house slammed shut. The conversation was terminated, but the seed was sown.

Geoff continued to shovel earth for a full ten minutes before he heard the back door swing open again, and he saw Pete re-emerge with two steaming cups of coffee. It was now dark, and the two men stood in the chill night air and drank their coffee. The lights from the house cast eerie shadows across the lawn.

Geoff cupped his hands around the steaming drink. 'Something very strange happened to me today.'

'Strange?' Pete muttered, his tall figure silhouetted against the house. 'I've just had my house ransacked.' He sighed. 'Okay, I'll bite, what strange thing happened to you today?'

'I got zapped. By the Holy Spirit.'

'So you're now an arm-waving, tongue-speaking,

hand-clapping raving loonie, like the rest of them?'
Pete's voice was heavy with sarcasm.

'Nope. I just realised that there was no way I
could take on the needs of Redbrook on my own.
I've only been here a few days... and I felt like I
had nothing more to give.'

'Maybe you just needed a couple of days rest.'
Pete began to sound more sympathetic.

'Or maybe I needed to understand that I just
haven't got enough strength and love to go round.'

Pete slurped back the last dregs of his coffee.
'Let's bury the cat. I fear you've got a sermon
coming on.'

'I have, Pete... and it's just for you and Jill. I
hope you'll be there on Sunday morning to hear it.'

'Okay,' he replied 'But on one condition.'

'And what's that?'

'That you and Sarah stay for dinner. I'm a dab
hand at lasagne.'

The two men lowered the cat into its grave. It
was a strangely solemn experience and they stood
silently and respectfully for a moment. At last Pete
coughed in a slightly embarrassed manner. 'Er,
Geoff, you know I don't really hold much for formal
prayers, but it somehow wouldn't seem right if we
just... Would you say a quick one?'

Geoff nodded, touched at the tall man's obvious
sense of loss.

After Geoff had prayed the prayer and covered
the grave the two men walked solemnly back to the
house.

'What was the cat's name?' Geoff asked.

Pete turned and smiled. 'His name was Lucky.'

It was dark by the time that the Express Coach pulled in to Digbeth Coach Station in Birmingham and Dave disembarked. He ambled up the long busy road towards the city centre clutching tight the soft black bag which contained all his worldly possessions and also some of Pete and Jill's. He felt cold and miserable.

He walked past St. Martins Church and into the Bull Ring shopping complex. Many of the shops were already locked and shuttered, and for some time he stood in a doorway and watched the home-bound commuters rushing past. Everyone seemed to have somewhere to go, except for him.

All evening he walked, and stood, and watched. He found a bar at the back of New Street Station, and passed more than an hour hiding in a corner and drinking four pints of beer. His mind filled with technicolour freeze-frames from his morning of frenzied destruction.

His feeling of misery was indescribable. Last night he slept in a good clean bed, ate all he wanted and watched TV. Tonight he had nothing but a few clothes, £200 in cash and some stolen rings and necklaces. He took the money out of his bag and counted it on the table before him.

He stuffed it back in the bag again and wrapped his coat around him before venturing out into the cold night air. He thought about booking in at a cheap hotel, but he was scared that someone might recognise him. He'd have to give identification, and that was always difficult.

He walked around the station concourse, sat on a bench beside the empty platform for a while, and watched the Inter-City expresses pull in and out.

Everyone was going somewhere, but his life was permanently 'in transit'.

He began to wonder why Pete and Jill had taken him in at all; and how Jill was dealing with the loss of her precious cat. He wondered whether Geoff Notes had reported his absence to the police... and if, even now, they were searching Waterloo in order to bring him to court. He shuddered in the chill of the night air, and began to feel very cold.

Geoff and Pete were not searching Waterloo, they were tucking in to a large plate of lasagne. Sarah was eating, too, but Jill declined. She still felt nauseous after the events of the day. But she sat with them, nursing one of the cats and staring thoughtfully at the candle in the centre of the table.

They talked about a lot of things. At first the topics were general: surviving in London, decorating, and the state of the Methodist connexion. Then the conversation moved on to things closer to home and in particular the divisions within their own church. Even as recently as yesterday Geoff would have naturally sided with Pete and Jill on matters connected with the Holy Spirit. The self-absorption of some of the big charismatic churches had not gone unnoticed by Geoff and his more liberal colleagues. Their concerns about gifts and manifestations often seemed to blind them to what was going on outside their church doors. But as Geoff told them of his experience in Adam's flat it became clear that something had happened to him that could not easily be explained. Geoff had not been whooped up into an emotional frenzy by a skilled evangelist at an evangelical rally, he had been more than a little depressed and sitting in a council flat. Sarah looked at Geoff thoughtfully as he described the renewing power of the Holy Spirit. She felt sad that she hadn't been there to share the moment with him.

Jill was gently stroking the cat's head, and was still feeling distressed. At last she put the cat down and sipped her glass of wine. 'What's your spiritual experience got to do with the real world, Geoff? It sounds like some sort of escapism to me.'

Geoff put down his knife and fork, wiped his mouth with the serviette and spoke quietly but earnestly. 'When I walked round Redbrook this morning I was all for packing the ministry in. I've been giving out since the moment I arrived here, and I felt like I'd nothing left to give.'

'So what's changed?' Jill held the wine glass to her lips.

'I've realised that it can't be done in our strength. We need God's. We've not got enough love to go round... but God can supply it.'

Geoff took up the knife and fork again. 'If you really want to care for Dave, you'll need a strength of love and compassion beyond anything you can find in yourself. That's why Jesus said he'd send us a 'Helper'—the Holy Spirit.'

'But I don't want to talk gibberish and sing silly choruses all the time. Isn't it all part of the same package?' Jill turned the glass gently round.

'Look, Jill' Geoff spoke enthusiastically through a mouthful of lasagne, 'all this is new to me. All that I know is that God's power is for real... and we all need it. Okay?'

'I think we're going to need that power to go on

helping Dave, 'there's no way I can forgive him in my own strength.' She looked at Pete. 'How about you?'

'I've been a Christian for a long time, but my Christianity is very cerebral—I can't handle emotion. But if God's power is about making us more effective down here... and not some emotional trip in the clouds... then I want it. If God's power can help us to help Dave... even better.' Pete swept back his hair.

The plates were empty and the candle was burning low, but conversation continued throughout the evening and into the night. At 11 o'clock Geoff suggested that he pray for them, and for a long time all four sat silently around the table, bathing in the presence of God's love. It was a healing, renewing experience... and very real.

Dave walked aimlessly on through the dark streets of Birmingham, until at last he found a multi-story car-park half full of cars. He made his way to the fourth storey, and to a darkened corner furthest from the lift. He took an extra jumper out of his bag and put it on, then wedged himself into the corner behind a car and fell asleep.

Dave awoke suddenly in agony and panic. Someone had just kicked him in the stomach. Then there were other kicks, and a hail of blows to his face. Three men were laughing hysterically. If the men thought that they had found an easy target they were soon to realise their mistake. Dave was an experienced fighter, and he knew how to inflict pain quickly and efficiently. He lashed out with his foot and smashed it into the knee-cap of one of his assailants before clambering unsteadily to his feet. As their mate folded to the floor screaming in pain the other two took stock of the situation. They had planned to have some fun at some unfortunate's expense, they had not intended to get hurt themselves. They were furious that they should be resisted so effectively. One of them threw himself at Dave and knocked him backwards into the wall, another grabbed Dave by the hair and cracked his head against the concrete. The injured man yelled at them to 'Kill the bastard' as they rained blows into Dave's body and face. Exhausted and drunken, Dave was no match for his attackers. He did his best to fend them off but they were too angry and too savage for him. Dave was a good fighter but was quickly overcome by the sheer ferocity of the angry young men. The dark figures pushed him to the floor again and kicked him all the more aggressively. He was in excruciating agony.

After some moments the kicking ceased. The last thing Dave saw was the three men running away with his coat and his soft bag, and then he slipped into unconsciousness. Dave lay there for more than two hours, until a sleepy security guard ambled through the car-park and shone his torch on the blood-spattered face of Dave Wilson.

The telephone beside Geoff's bed rang at 4:30 am, and he woke with a start. He glanced at the illuminated numerals of the digital alarm and blinked. Instantly he suspected trouble at Intensive Care, perhaps Ben had taken a turn for the worse.

'Hello, Rev Geoffrey Notes of Redbrook?'

'Yes, yes... that's me.'

'I'm sorry to bother you at this time of night sir, but we've got a badly concussed young man here... and we have no trace of identity except your name and address on a piece of paper in his trouser pocket. He's in his early twenties... with dark hair.'

'His name is Dave Wilson... the court has placed him in my keeping. Where is he, Charing Cross hospital?'

'No sir, he's at Birmingham General.'

'I'll come as soon as I can.' Geoff dressed quickly. Sarah peeked her face over the quilt.

'What on earth are you doing at this time in the morning?'

'It's Dave, he's in Birmingham General Hospital. He's been injured. Could you ask Adam to lead the prayer meeting this morning?'

Sarah sat up in bed. 'I hope everything goes okay.'

He kissed her gently on the cheek and crept downstairs so that he wouldn't disturb Rosie. Just as he was putting his coat on he noticed the glow of a cigarette in the darkness of the lounge. 'Hello, Rosie, is that you?'

'Yes, Geoff, I couldn't sleep. Thinking about Dave.'

'They've just phoned from Birmingham, I'm afraid. He's been injured. I'm going to see him now.'

'Hang on a minute,' Rosie whispered, stubbing out her cigarette, 'I'm coming too.' In a matter of minutes the two of them were driving through the heart of London towards the M40 and Birmingham. Geoff felt deep inside that this could be an important visit, and as he drove he prayed for wisdom.

By the time that Geoff and Rosie arrived at the 'General' Dave was out of the 'Accident and Emergency' room and 'under observation' in a small single side-ward. He was still very dazed. A young policeman was seated at his bedside.

Geoff and Rosie were shown into the room and they pulled up chairs beside the bed. Geoff looked at the young policeman. 'What's the score?'

'He's had a nasty beating. More than your average punch up. I'm just hoping he'll come through this without any permanent damage.' From the number of stitches evident on Dave's face that looked doubtful.

It was seven am, and Geoff, Rosie and the policeman sat for the next hour talking politely, and waiting for Dave to respond. Little did they know how earnestly they were being prayed for back at Redbrook church.

Adam was leading the meeting and most of the intercessions were for Ben, but Sarah's brief resumé of all that had happened to Pete and Jill, and Geoff's sudden departure for Birmingham, stirred others to offer prayer who had previously remained silent.

At precisely 7:45 am Pete prayed a fervent prayer for Dave, asking that whatever his condition... he might find healing and renewal. Jill responded with a loud 'Amen.'

At precisely 7:45 am Dave opened his eyes and looked around him in astonishment. A policeman, a minister, an ex-girlfriend... and closed his eyes again, hoping they might just disappear. 'Oh God,' he thought, 'haven't I been through enough?' He opened his eyes again; they were still there. Evidently not.

Chapter Eight

After the prayer meeting had finished Sarah and Margaret Briggs were left to wash up the coffee cups as usual. There was so much to talk about, but they were strangely silent. The beautiful atmosphere of the prayer meeting lingered in the air. After the last cup had been stacked Margaret broke the silence.

'Would you like some breakfast, Sarah? I don't expect that Geoff and Rosie will be back for hours yet.'

Sarah had planned her day exactly, and had estimated that if she worked all morning she could finish decorating the bedroom by lunchtime. She sighed inwardly as she recognised that it wasn't to be.

'Of course, Margaret. I'd like that.'

Ms Briggs solemnly locked the church and the two women walked briskly through the littered recreation ground, past the three tall tower blocks, and into a quiet cul-de-sac of suburban semis.

Margaret's house was exceedingly plain and joyless to Sarah's eye, and she struggled to find anything positive to say about the decor. The only overtly decorative features were stained glass panels in the top corners of the windows which had survived the onslaught of double glazing salesmen and remained untouched since the early nineteen thirties when the house had been built. Margaret was obviously a book person, and the lounge contained eight shelves of novels of varying shapes and sizes. A goodly number of them were thrillers with titles by Ian Fleming, Alastair McClean, and Jack Higgins in abundance. A large three bar electric fire with a pathetic 'coal flame' effect dominated the room.

'Sit down here, Sarah. I'll bring the breakfast in.' Margaret said firmly.

Sarah sat toward the fire warming her hands, and watching the bars spark and crackle in the damp atmosphere. The 'coal flame' effect buzzed irritatingly.

Sarah noticed a large pile of records in the corner of the room beside a sixties style walnut cabinet which contained one of the earliest stereo systems. Sarah went over to the records and flicked through the album sleeves. Margaret was obviously 'into' the classics.

'Bizet: 'Carmen Suite, The Toreador' by the Adelaide Symphony Orchestra; 'Brahms: Violin Concerto in D' by the Vienna Concert Orchestra: 'Tchaikovsky: Symphony no 6 in B major' by the Paris Philharmonic. It was all a strange world to Sarah Notes, whose music tastes ranged from Lloyd Webber to Cliff Richard.

At last Margaret entered with a neatly arranged tray containing a bowl of porridge, a boiled egg in a pretty china egg-cup, two slices of toast, a tiny pot of honey and a milky cup of coffee. The tray had folding metal legs and was soon transformed into a coffee table. Margaret returned with a similar tray-table for herself which was arranged in an identical way.

Sarah didn't feel like eating any of it, but she did her best to struggle appreciatively through each course. It was an effort not to grimace as she sipped the coffee. Ms Briggs, like many of her generation, seemed to think that coffee made with lots of boiled milk was something of a treat. Conversation was evidently not flowing, so Margaret put down her egg cup and filled the awkward silence with a record by the Lincoln Cathedral choir.

A solemn and classical rendition of 'Out of the deep' (a setting of Psalm 130) filled the air. It was strangely beautiful, but Sarah found such heavy music hard to cope with so early in the morning. The words of the counter-tenor filled the room.

'From the depths of my despair I call to you, Lord. Hear my cry, O Lord; listen to my call for help.'

Sarah couldn't help but think that this record summed up what Margaret Briggs was actually feeling; and she began to see that the woman's bright and cheery attitude at church over the last few mornings was masking a mood of deep despair.

Both women continued to eat breakfast in silence until, some twenty minutes later, the final solo faded and the needle clicked noisily over the plastic buffers in the centre of the record. Margaret got up and moved the delicate stereo arm back to its holder. The automatic return had long ceased to work.

Sarah put down her coffee cup... 'Does that sum up where you're at, Margaret?'

'What do you mean?' she asked, defensively.

'In the depths... the depths of despair?' Sarah wasn't sure where this line of questioning might lead, and she was acutely aware of the age difference between them. Margaret might feel uncomfortable talking to someone so much younger than herself. Nevertheless she instinctively felt that there was a story to be told here, a story that Margaret needed to tell.

Margaret placed the record gently back into its sleeve and sat back down in her high back easy chair. She leant forward to feel the soothing warmth of the fire.

'I've lived in this house all my life... all fifty-four years of it. Of course, it was a different area in the old days. One of London's most desirable garden suburbs. Nearly everyone who lived here worked in the City, my father worked at the head office of the bankers called Coutts.'

Margaret paused thoughtfully, but Sarah didn't interrupt. It was clear that Margaret had planned what to say and that it would be unhelpful to interrupt her monologue.

'I always wanted to work in the Civil Service, right from being a child. You could say I was brought up to it. Of course, when I first went in, women didn't stand much chance of promotion. So, after my short course at the secretarial college, the Civil Service started me off in the typing pool.

'I was so ambitious, Sarah. I worked so hard. I was determined to be one of the first women to break out of the pathetic subservience of the typing pool. I studied at night school, I took exams, I worked overtime... I was always the one willing to do the boring job... anything, to get noticed.

'Well I did get noticed, by a senior Civil Servant a lot older than me, a real high flyer on his way to the top floor. Anyway, to cut a long story short, we had an affair. It was a rather pathetic shabby affair, in hindsight, but nevertheless he was the great love of my life.

'Of course, he was married, three children—all at boarding school; and a demanding wife who nagged him unmercifully... a bored suburban woman with little to do, except make her husband's life a misery. At least that is how I thought of her.'

Sarah's eyes widened in disbelief. She'd have categorised Margaret Briggs as 'forever a spinster'; this upright pillar of the local community didn't look the type for an illicit love affair.

'It lasted for more than ten years. I was the perfect mistress, he knew that he could trust me to be discreet. My parents were ailing and it was miserable, here at home. My relationship with David kept me alive.

'He gave me my love of music. We went to concerts every week, usually on a Wednesday... and over the years he introduced me to the classics. It enriched my life, Sarah, I'll always owe him for that. He was my friend as well as my lover. I never asked him to leave his wife, I knew he wouldn't, but I believe he loved me almost as much as I loved him.

'But then he began to lose weight... got very tired, was absent from work. The usual story... he'd been a heavy smoker... lung cancer.' Margaret's voice wavered with emotion, and she paused for a moment to compose herself.

'It was the most difficult time of my life, Sarah. I loved him so much, but I couldn't even see him. I managed a few visits into the hospital, but I was always frightened that his wife would suspect.

'And the funeral... I was there as a representative of the department. And trying not to cry too much, and wondering if anyone had guessed.'

Sarah moved gently to Margaret's side, sat on the floor beside her, and took her hand. The older woman's eyes were glistening with tears. 'I've never told anyone all this, Sarah... and I hope you'll keep it all to yourself. I know you will.'

Sarah nodded in agreement. Her heart beat faster with the sense of responsibility she carried in this sacred moment of confession.

'Since he died I've been torn apart by guilt, and regret... and yet also by gratitude, because my life would have been so much poorer without him. So I threw everything into my work again... and every evening... the music. I re-lived those concerts... and I've missed him so much.

'But now I'm redundant. Finished. It's all gone. And, well Sarah, I feel like my life is over. These last few days I've thought seriously about... well, you know...'

There was silence. The enormity of Margaret's confession overwhelmed Sarah. She would never have imagined a good old stalwart like Margaret as being a potential victim of suicide.

'And your faith... the church? Doesn't that help?'

Margaret wiped a tear from her cheek. 'Oh, down there I'm just "good old Ms Briggs"... always to be relied upon. A pillar of the place to keep the minutes and do the locking up. Don't get me wrong, I've enjoyed it and they're nice people... but I've always seen my Christianity as something practical to get on and do. I've not been one for great spiritual experiences.'

And then, as suddenly as the great door to Margaret Briggs' inner being had swung open, it swung shut again. She took a deep breath, drew herself upright in the chair and returned to her normal cheery self.

'Well, that's my story, dear. We've both got a lot to do today.' She picked up Sarah's breakfast tray and marched to the kitchen. Sarah followed with the other tray, but before she could enter the kitchen Margaret had returned and taken it from her.

'Shall we talk again?' Sarah asked, almost pleadingly.

'Maybe, my dear. But you've got enough on your plate without worrying about an old moaner like me.' Ms Briggs held the front door open and smiled. 'Thanks for coming, Sarah; and thanks for listening.'

Before she could reply Sarah found herself outside in the cold chill air with the door shut firmly behind her. She felt an utter failure—there had been so much she wanted to say.

She walked thoughtfully home, praying earnestly that God would give her another opportunity to share with the mysterious Margaret Briggs. She could only hope that the older woman wouldn't do anything stupid in the meantime.

Sarah walked briskly to the manse, pulling up the collar of her coat to give her some protection from the biting wind. She was already two hours adrift with her decorating schedule, but knew that if she worked all afternoon without stopping for lunch, she could still finish painting the bedroom by teatime.

She turned the corner of the terrace and walked briskly to the door of number 32. Within minutes she was perched at the top of the ladder splashing paint over the long wall. The bright music from a favourite compact disc filled the air, but the noise didn't drown the uncomfortable thoughts that echoed round her mind. Sarah Notes had never heard a confession before, and the responsibility bore heavily upon her.

Geoff and Rosie arrived at 1pm with steaming bags of fish and chips. 'Luncheon is served,' he shouted to Sarah upstairs, knowing that she would be decorating.

The greasy meal was laid out on plates, and a plastic cup of mushy peas poured out onto each plate. Sarah let her paint roller drip over the tray, and then placed it gently on an outspread newspaper on the floor.

The three sat and ate in the kitchen, though Sarah barely touched her meal: she was still full from breakfast. Geoff was full of excitement because of his early morning jaunt to Birmingham, and described in graphic detail all that had happened to Dave. Rosie was excited, too, and longed to tell

Sarah of her hopes for a renewal of her relationship with Dave. 'He needs me to look after him now. Before, it was always me needing him.'

Sarah was very distant, however, and sat at the kitchen table looking out of the window at the looming flats on the skyline. Her thoughts were still full of the inner revelations of one Margaret Briggs.

'And how was your morning, darling?' Geoff said at last, deliberately trying not to sound patronising, 'Is the back bedroom finished?'

'No,' Sarah sighed, 'I've had a rather busy morning.'

'What's been happening? Anything I should know about? Don't tell me someone else is pregnant?' He looked at Rosie who grinned back. 'Ms Briggs perhaps.'

'Nothing like that. Now I must get back to the decorating. Any assistance would be greatly appreciated.'

And so a few minutes later all three of them, dressed in old clothes, had taken up the rollers and attacked the shabby walls of the back bedroom. They were moving quickly and methodically, and Sarah's spirits were rising as she realised she might get the room finished in good time, after all.

About 2:30pm the door-knocker thudded loudly. Geoff raced downstairs, wiped his sticky painted hands on his old shirt, and pulled open the heavy door. His heart sank. Standing there was Adam, beaming from ear to ear, and a very tall bronzed man in a white suit with a stetson hat on his head. He was carrying a small red brief case.

'Good morning Pastor. Praise the Lord!' smiled

Adam, 'Have you got a few moments to see us? Doctor Nodder was in town, so he came to visit.'

Geoff smiled politely, and welcomed both men into the lounge. The immaculately dressed American sat in the armchair, removed his stetson hat, and gazed sympathetically at the paint splattered minister.

Geoff looked askance at the tall American, fixing his eyes on the peculiar silk tie-band which was fixed in a neat bow. The Texan crossed his legs, revealing boots which had evidently been made for equestrian use. The strong sweet smell of after-shave filled the air.

'Well, it's a joy to meet you, Doctor Notes.' drawled the American. 'Please let me introduce myself. I'm the President of the Rainbow Arch Ministry Team and Healing Confederation.' He dug into his back trouser pocket and pulled out a gold embossed business card with a colourful rainbow stamped on it.

'I was just passing through London on my way to Paris. I'm scheduled to speak at the new American Community Church which services the employees of EuroDisney. I thought I'd just call in to see brother Adam, here, who's been expressing an interest in our Crusade package for some time.' The American smiled broadly, revealing a gold tooth.

Geoffrey Notes felt completely out of his depth. 'What kind of package did you have in mind?'

The American clicked open his brief case and pulled out three shiny gold folders, each with the rainbow insignia. The three men opened the presentation packs and flicked through the loose leaf portfolio which they contained.

'First of all, Doctor Notes, let's talk about the embarrassing subject of money. I want to put your mind at rest. This Crusade package comes at no cost to your supporters, it will be totally sponsored by my friends in Texas. It comes to you as an expression of our love for the Christians in the Old Country. Of course we will provide the good people of Redbrook with opportunities to thank God for his mercy by contributing to the work of my organisation around the world.'

Geoff was impressed by the offer. His experience of missions was limited, but he knew that they could turn out expensive. He looked through the portfolio at the beautiful colour pictures of Doctor Nodder addressing collegiate students, air force personnel, Congressmen at a prayer breakfast, and a football stadium full of Brazilians.

Then there was a 'media profile', showing Doctor Nodder with his wife and six children. They were all seated on white horses in front of a ranch. There were shots of the 'Doctor Nodder Dallas Retreat Centre', which had three swimming pools and a landscaped golf-course. It looked like a rather up-market Holiday Inn.

'Oh yes, Geoff,' the American smiled warmly, 'if you decided to go with the mission we'd love for you and your good wife to come and visit us at the Retreat Centre... at our expense, of course... to help you to prepare for the mission.' Geoff's eyes widened in anticipation. He'd always wanted to visit the States.

'Mm,' Geoff pondered, 'but you must understand, this isn't my decision... it's up to the whole church. They'd all have to be sure that this mission

was the most effective way of reaching the neigh-
bourhood.'

'Well of course,' the American smiled again,
'that's why I've brought you our video presentation. I'd like you to show it to your congregation
and let them decide. Then you can fax my office
with the result and we'll schedule some dates.'

It all sounded very easy, but Geoff could tell that
the American was looking at things through rainbow tinted spectacles. He certainly couldn't com-
prehend the multi-coloured spectrum of theological
opinion at Redbrook community church. Geoff
knew that there was some distance between Inner
London Methodism and the Texan Bible belt.

Without warning, the American sank to his knees
and clasped his hands together. He looked upward
to heaven as he prayed a long meandering prayer,
which took in the needs of 'the dark continent of
Europe held tight in Satan's grip'. Doctor Nodder
asked the Lord to confirm the plans for the
Redbrook mission in the hearts of Geoffrey Notes
and his congregation. Geoff echoed the Amen, and
just restrained himself from praying for 'the dark
State of Texas held tight in Satan's grip'.

Adam escorted Doctor Nodder to the door, and
after the Texan had placed his stetson on his head
he turned and stared at Geoff with sharp blue eyes.
'I've a strong feeling that I'll be seeing much more
of you, Pastor,' and he shook Geoff's hand with
such conviction that Geoff flinched in pain. Geoff
returned to the decorating and Sarah remarked
how the strong smell of after-shave had permeated
the whole house.

It was late evening before Geoff arrived at the

General to see Ben. It had been a very long day since the unexpected 'phone call at 4:30am and the rush to Birmingham. Geoff's arm was still aching from the afternoon with the paint roller, and he sensed a lingering numbness in his fingers from Pastor Nodder's handshake.

He walked slowly up the long corridor toward the intensive care cubicle hoping above hope that there might be some improvement in Ben's critical condition. Geoff pushed open the plastic doors but froze at the sight before him.

A young doctor in a white coat was barking instructions to several nurses and a colleague in a green operating theatre suit. The 'crash' trolley was in use, and they were desperately trying to revive Ben by pumping surges of electricity into his silent heart. The intensity of concentration among all those present was such that none of them even noticed Geoff's arrival.

He stepped inside and the plastic door flap closed behind him. The 'crash' team got more agitated and desperate by the second. They were racing against time, and every second that passed increased the odds against them. Geoff stood motionless and watched their staccato movements and stern expressions. He held his breath and prayed.

One of the monitors showed a blip of response, and the team hurried on, renewed by this small glimmer of hope. A full twenty minutes they struggled, and shouted, and watched... and then, quite suddenly, the young doctor pulled off his plastic gloves, threw them to the floor and sighed, 'I'm calling it a day. Nurse, mark the time. It's over. We've lost him.'

The dull bleep of the monitor alarm continued for a few seconds, and then, at last, someone turned it off. For a brief moment everything was still, and the crash team stood in silence... as if to assimilate what had just happened, and then they began to pack away their equipment.

Geoff slipped out of the cubicle and walked thoughtfully down the corridor, half wondering where to go or what to do. As he passed the green carpeted waiting room he glanced in and saw Miriam seated beside Margaret Briggs. The two women were sat silently staring at the carpet, and waiting for news.

Geoff slipped inside and knelt before them. With his right hand he grasped Miriam's hand, and with his left, Margaret's. 'I have come to tell you that Ben's suffering is over, and that the Lord has come to take him. The doctors did everything that they could, but little Ben had suffered enough, and, well... it's over.'

Miriam gazed deep into Geoff's eyes in disbelief. 'But Geoff, it couldn't be... not after we prayed. It couldn't be.' She uttered a haunting heart-rending wail of grief, and Margaret and Geoff held her as she sobbed great cries of despair. The young doctor in the white coat stood in the doorway and felt completely inadequate. He was relieved that Geoff was there.

Over an hour later, when Miriam was somewhat more composed, Margaret and Geoff supported her, one on either arm, on the long walk to Ben's cubicle. Geoff pushed open the flaps, and was relieved to see that all of the machinery was gone.

Ben lay, as if asleep, on a pure white pillow. Miriam held the small limp body close to her and whispered words of love to her only child. Margaret and Geoff stood close by and prayed with an anguish too deep for words. Geoff marvelled that here... even here... perhaps, especially here... in this dark shadowland of sorrow... he could sense the presence of the great Shepherd of the sheep.

Chapter Nine

The morning after Ben's death Geoffrey Notes sat
at his kitchen table staring into his coffee cup. He
looked ashen and depressed, and Sarah wondered if
anything would shift the dark mood that overshadowed him.

'I need your help, Geoff... and I need it today.'
Sarah poured herself a second cup of coffee.

Geoff turned to her and stared, as if looking
through a haze. 'Of course, darling...' Some mind-
less decorating was just what he needed. Perhaps it
would give him the time to work out what he should
have done when handling this terrible situation.
Where he went wrong.

'Today, Geoff, is 'Blue Cross Day' in the January
sales... and today is the day we blow the last of our
savings on a decent bed.'

Geoff rolled his eyes in despair. 'What, today? I
really can't face it, love.'

'Oh yes you can. Blue Cross Day comes but once
a year, and we're not going to sleep another year on

that heap of old iron from the jumble sale.' Sarah's voice was hard and uncompromising.

'Must I?' there was a pathetic note of pleading in his voice reminiscent of a little boy who didn't want to go shopping with his mother.

'Yes Geoff, you may not recognize it, but you're at breaking point. It'll do you good.'

Geoff couldn't think of a less effective remedy for stress than the January sales but didn't have the energy to fight. He trailed meekly to the car, wallet in hand, hoping that this great shopping expedition would soon be over.

His mind was still full of the events of the previous night, and although he knew that he was emotionally exhausted he felt guilty that he wasn't spending the day with Miriam.

Before long Geoff and Sarah were embroiled in the annual scrummage for rock-bottom bargains in the last tussle of the January sales. The sales assistants were overwhelmed, and had little time for anything other than to stripe credit cards and stick 'sold' labels onto the merchandise in their domain.

Sarah was in a crazy mood. The depression and grief of recent days were really getting to her. She wanted to be alive again, and she wanted Geoff to herself... just for a little while.

'There's no way that I'm going to buy a bed that I'm going to be unhappy with for the next fifteen years, so we'll have to test them all.' Sarah was uncompromising again.

'What do you mean?' Geoff looked worried.

'We sort of jump on them.'

'Jump on them?' Geoff looked aghast.

'Like this,' Sarah giggled, and leapt spread-eagled onto a 'Rhapsody' king-size bed which seemed to fill a whole corner of the showroom.

Geoffrey Notes flushed with embarrassment.

'Come on, Geoff, try it.'

Geoff looked furtively around him, and when fully assured that no-one was looking he leapt onto the other side of the bed.

'No good, Geoff. It's too soft, and anyway… the headboard's dark and boring.'

Next in line was a luxury 'Nimbus Cloud' divan. Sarah gave it the same treatment, this time with even more vigour. Geoff followed. 'No good.' she declared 'Too hard… and very common-looking.'

The next bed was marked 'Prelude' and described on a large cardboard display-stand as 'elegant with a touch of drama'. It was reduced by 55% in the sale. The bed looked attractive to Sarah, and the price looked good to Geoff.

'This time we'll give it the full works. Both together… after three.' Sarah held his hand, and they both leapt.

The bed collapsed with an enormous crash, the headboard flying one way and the base-board hitting the floor like a clap of thunder. Geoff and Sarah landed in a heap giggling hysterically and uncontrollably. All of the intense grief and emotion of the previous hours poured out in their shrieks of laughter.

Geoff opened his eyes and looked in dismay at the crowd of watching shoppers who had seemingly assembled from nowhere, and who were laughing, too.

A very superior floor manager materialised

beside them and asked helpfully, 'Is everything alright?'

'I think we've got a screw loose,' retorted Sarah, untangling herself from Geoff.

'I didn't like to say,' replied the manager dryly. 'Were you thinking of buying a bed or merely destroying one?'

'We were thinking of buying, but we don't like this one, it's broken.'

'Perhaps if I threw in a screwdriver you might like to take it off my hands?'

And so Geoff and Sarah bought the 'Prelude', partly through the embarrassment of what had happened... and partly because the floor manager offered them a further 25% discount in view of the freshly scratched headboard. Geoff remarked that the Lord moved in mysterious ways, but the salesman didn't seem particularly impressed.

Delighted with their purchase, and united in a common sense of 'joie de vivre', they took the lift to the top floor of the department store and treated themselves to coffee and cheesecake.

'I haven't laughed so much in ages,' Geoff smiled, a moustache of cream covering his upper lip.

'I know, Geoff... isn't that sad?' Sarah was deadly serious. 'You haven't been the Geoff Notes I married since you came here. You've lost your sparkle... your mad view of life. You're becoming a 'grey' person, full of the cares of the world, and it frightens me, Geoff.'

Geoff sipped his coffee. 'A divided church, a dying kid, a pregnant homeless girl, a vandalised home... you've got to admit, it has been a bit heavy.'

'That's London, Geoff, you knew it would be like this. But you can't carry the cares of the world on your shoulders all the time, it'll destroy you.'

'What do I do then... laugh, and the whole world laughs with me?' He sounded sarcastic.

'No, Geoff... but you've got to learn how to live in peace.'

'Easier said than done,' there was a quiver of emotion in his voice. 'Everyone looks to me for support. I'm the stable, reliable, dependable guy who's always there and who never crumbles. But who cares about me? Whose shoulder do I cry on?'

Sarah smiled warmly. 'Mine.'

'But Sarah... many of these things are too painful for me to bear... I can't unload them on to you.'

'Try me.'

'But you weren't called to the ministry... I was. It's not your job. It's mine.'

'But God called me to be your wife, Geoff... and if I am to support you, you've got to let me into some of your pain.'

Geoff looked at Sarah, and loved her. He was grateful that, in the painful work of caring, he knew for sure that someone cared for him. 'Promise me something,' he asked as he finished the last of his cheesecake.

'Anything.' Sarah looked serious.

'If I ever look like I'm becoming too dull or grey, or if I'm taking myself too seriously, take me shopping and make me bounce on a bit of furniture.'

'Well we do need a new settee,' grinned Sarah mischievously. Inside she was intensely relieved, this was the man she had fallen in love with and married.

Six days later Redbrook community church was filled to capacity for Ben's funeral. It was a real community occasion, with representatives from Ben's school, the Intensive Care Unit at the Hospital, and the tower block where Miriam and Ben lived.

The church had turned out in force too; and Pip's uniformed cub pack sat together in the front row. There wasn't a seat to spare, and Geoff peeked through the vestry door in amazement as he watched the crowd flocking in to the church.

He felt very nervous. He hadn't been able to eat any breakfast or lunch—and although he'd sat at his study desk for hours on end he hadn't been able to find anything suitable to say.

Margaret Briggs looked at her watch. 'It's 2:25pm, Geoff; I think it's time you went outside to meet the cortege.'

She prayed a simple but meaningful prayer asking God to give Geoff 'the right words' to say. Geoff wondered if she'd noticed that the sheet of paper headed 'Sermon' was still completely blank.

Geoff stood outside and glanced up at the leaden overcast sky as the hearse and two black limousines edged their way slowly up the road toward the front of the church. A wave of emotion swept over him as he remembered Ben's small black face on the white pillow. He'd never heard his voice, never spoken to him, nor really known the child. What right had he to speak at the funeral? He felt totally inadequate. The hearse gently cruised to a halt outside the church, and the black-clad mourners formed into a line.

Margaret Briggs pushed open the double-fronted doors to the church as the organist played the last strains of the well known tune 'Crimond'. Turning briefly behind him to check that the procession was ready, Geoff opened his prayer book and chanted the familiar words.

'I am the resurrection and the life...'

The small white coffin was wheeled on a trolley by Adam, representing the Sunday School, and Pip, who was dressed in her Scout uniform. They firmly held the gold handles at waist height and pulled the coffin along as they walked solemnly forward.

Behind them came Miriam, standing proud and erect, and with an expression of serenity which spoke of inner peace. Adam's wife supported her on one arm, and Margaret Briggs on the other. Other distant members of Miriam's family followed on... and then, at the rear of the sad procession came Bert and his faithful guide dog. (Bert had in fact arrived late for the funeral and wasn't really aware that he was part of the procession. But no-one seemed to mind.)

Geoff made his way to the lectern as the white coffin gently came to rest at the communion rail. The congregation sat down. Geoff stared out at the packed church and was aware that every eye was on him. Everyone was looking to him for some shred of comfort, some glimmer of hope. He only wished he had some to give.

'Thank-you for coming here today. We've come to support a grieving mother, Miriam. We've come to celebrate the life of a young child, Ben. We've come to hold hands together in the face of over-whelming tragedy. But most of all, we've come to worship God... whose ways are higher than our ways and whose comfort and strength far surpass our own.'

Geoff opened his hymnbook and gulped back the grief he was fighting. 'Many of our hymns were written at times of great tragedy. Joseph Scriven wrote these words when his fiancée died, just before their marriage. I pray that they may bring the same comfort to us that they did to him.'

The congregation stood and with a surprisingly joyous rhythm they sang together.

> What a Friend we have in Jesus,
> All our sins and griefs to bear!
> What a privilege to carry
> Everything to God in prayer!
> O what peace we often forfeit,
> O what needless pain we bear,
> All because we do not carry
> Everything to God in prayer!

Margaret Briggs, standing close beside Miriam, listened intently as the younger woman sang out the familiar words with her strong West Indian accent. She had sung the hymn a thousand times... but never listened to the words so intently.

Her mind was not on Ben, nor even on the grieving mother beside her... but on her own acute depression, on the loss of the man she loved and the ending of the job which had been her life.

How could Miriam sing these words with such assurance... such certainty? How could this younger woman, whose loss was so much greater than her own, press on with such faith and conviction?

Her own voice was carried along by the voice of Miriam beside her, and she heard herself singing...

Have we trials and temptations?
Is there trouble anywhere?
We should never be discouraged;
Take it to the Lord in prayer.

As she sang the tears began to fall. It was the first time that she could remember crying since her childhood. Those who noticed assumed that they were tears for Ben, but in reality, they were tears of release... and even of joy.

Can we find a friend so faithful
Who will all our sorrows share?
Jesus knows our every weakness;
Take it to the Lord in prayer.

As Margaret Briggs mourned the loss of a small child, she found a way to mourn the loss of so many years of unfulfilled hopes and broken dreams. In that moment of deep sadness she discovered that there was, indeed, a Friend beside her.

Miriam's mind was full of happy pictures. She was re-running glimpses of her life with Ben... memories which gave her strength and comfort. She saw him taking his first steps, kicking a football at the recreation ground, running—lunchbox in hand—into the school-yard on his first day at school, marching with the cub pack after church parade... and seated proudly on his brand new bicycle...

In His arms He'll take and shield thee;
Thou wilt find a solace there.

Margaret and Miriam stood, hand in hand, facing the little white coffin with a strength which was beyond their own.

The service concluded and the congregation stood whilst the little procession slowly left the church. Only a handful of people went on with Geoff and Miriam and the family group to the graveside. The cortege drove through the large urban cemetery until, at last, they arrived at a small space between other graves, where Ben's final resting place had been neatly prepared.

The small white coffin was gently lowered into the hole, and Geoff solemnly whispered the familiar words...

'Ashes to ashes... dust to dust...'

Geoff returned to the funeral car with Miriam, whispering words of comfort as they went. Margaret hung behind awhile, looking at the white coffin deep in the earth. Sarah Notes was standing beside her.

'Come on, Margaret... we must leave him now...'

Margaret turned and smiled. 'Yes, I know.' There was a new softness in her voice. A new warmth in her eye.

'How are you, my dear?' Sarah whispered, holding the older woman by the arm as they walked past the rows of graves toward the funeral car.

'Fine, Sarah. I'm going to be fine, now. Really.'

Sarah clambered into the car beside her, and resisted the temptation to press the question further. Soon, Sarah Notes would see the change in Margaret's life... but would never know what had triggered it.

Pete and Jill, meanwhile, had left the church and were driving through the early afternoon rush-hour towards the M40. They were the kind of people who made spontaneous decisions, and this was just such an occasion.

Deep within them, though they hadn't recognised it, they were in the flux of profound change in their life together. Ben's death, as deaths often do, was a solemn reminder of the transience of life and the futility of much of what they had been living for.

They drove without speaking, a compact disc of Beethoven's Symphony no 6 filling the car with sound.

They turned off the busy M40 and followed the A423 northbound, turning off into the quaint village of Great Bourton. They had arrived in another world. They parked and strolled past thatched cottages and a babbling brook to the old village inn which had been tastefully transformed into a restaurant. A smell of wood-smoke from village chimneys filled the air.

They sat in the quaint old restaurant with its horsebrasses and roaring woodfire and browsed the menu. They both ordered soup and pasta from the uniformed waitress. The emotion of Ben's funeral was still very present, and they spoke in gentle,

hushed tones… as if unwilling to break the
atmosphere.

'Geoff's sermon was powerful.' Pete whispered.

'Mmm' Jill murmured.

'Inspired.'

'Mmm,' Jill looked at him, questioningly.

'If you don't receive the Kingdom of God like a
little child, you'll never enter it. I wish I could
believe like that… but I really don't think it's me…'

Jill gently unfolded the green linen serviette and
placed it on her knee. 'I don't think it means you've
got to commit intellectual suicide. I could never do
that, you know I couldn't… but perhaps, well,
perhaps besides all our arguing and philosophis-
ing… we need to trust Him more.'

'You'll never catch me waving my arms in the air
and dancing around. It's not in my character.' Pete
brushed his hair out of his eyes.

'Perhaps there are other ways of showing that
you trust Him.'

'Like?' Pete frowned at her.

'Like forgiving Dave… like taking him back…
like being willing to risk everything we've got…
like believing that Jesus is in it with us.'

'But I've not had any technicolour spiritual
experiences… no flashing lights in my head… no
walking on air type moments… I understand what
Geoff was telling us about, you know, at Adam's
flat, but I just can't imagine it happening to me.
I'm not sure I ever want to be that out of control.
But I really do want to know God is with me. Do
you think he ever gives his people down to earth
spiritual experiences?'

Jill looked softly at him. 'As the person who

knows you better than anyone else in the world I can honestly tell you... you're having one right now!'

Pete smiled a broad knowing grin. Indeed, she did know him all too well.

A pretty girl with bobbed hair who wore a name badge announcing her as 'Louise Burn' swung into the room with a tray bearing steaming bowls of soup. She smiled brightly as she served them. The conversation was over, but the atmosphere of relaxed familiarity continued. Pete and Jill had never been closer than they were during that meal.

They arrived at Birmingham General soon after the start of visiting time, and were shown in to a long public ward. Dave was half-way down the ward on the left hand side. He was sitting in bed and reading a newspaper.

Pete felt a distinct uneasiness as he approached Dave's bed. He wondered if he really could forgive this man who'd wrecked his house, and if indeed he could even bear to see him again.

Dave glimpsed round the corner of his newspaper and groaned, 'Oh my God, no.' He pulled the newspaper higher, hoping they might pass him by. They didn't.

Jill and Pete sat on the chairs beside Dave's bed and waited. At last, Dave lay the newspaper down and joked 'Well, hello there... what brings nice people like you to a dump like this?'

Pete looked at Dave with compassion. 'You do, my friend. You do.'

Jill felt suddenly very proud of her husband. It was nothing short of a miracle that Pete could speak in such a way. Jill awkwardly placed a box of chocolates on the bed.

'They're for you, Dave. With love from your middle-aged, middle-class suburban friends.'

Dave smirked. 'You haven't got any fags, have you? I'm really gasping.'

'Later, Dave, later.' Pete said reassuringly. 'But first, what are you going to do when you get out of here?'

'I think the vicar might help.' Dave ripped open the cellophane on the chocolate box and rustled through the packing to the chocolates beneath.

'We'd like you to come back to our place... if you want.' Jill looked at him almost pleadingly.

Dave smiled his cynical smile again. 'Cleared it up, now, have you?'

'Yes, it's all back together. Your room's waiting for you.'

Dave pushed a chocolate into his mouth and flinched, his top lip was still very swollen. 'I'm sorry about the cat. I just got a bit carried away. Didn't mean any harm, like.'

'Come home, Dave, as soon as you can,' Jill forced a smile, 'we'll be waiting for you.'

Dave took the chocolate out of his mouth and threw it in the bin. 'Ruddy ginger... what are they playing at? Day after tomorrow I come out... any chance of some help with the bus fare? It could take hours to hitch.'

Pete placed a crisp twenty-pound note on the bed. 'We'll see you soon then.' And with that, Pete and Jill made the long trek back to their car. They both felt strangely uneasy. Somehow things had not gone as they had imagined. It was as though Dave hadn't grasped the enormity of what he had done, nor how hard it was for them to forgive him.

Chapter Ten

A group of children were gathering on the corner a hundred yards or so from the chapel. Several of them were riding B.M.X. or mountain bikes, one or two were balancing on skate boards, the rest were on foot. The ubiquitous can was being kicked among them. One by one the gang came to perch on the low wall of one of the terraced house gardens. The chatter and the clattering finally became too much for the resident and he came charging out of his front door to shout at the group and move them on.

One of the boys was Danny, Adam's son. His father had no idea where he was. Quite frankly, Danny considered his father a major embarrassment. His fervent religious convictions served only to distance him from his streetwise son. The harder Adam exhorted Danny to 'shape up' and 'show some respect' the further he drove Danny away. The only time he went to church was when it could not be avoided—like the prayer meeting the other morning. Danny felt bad about Ben, he'd known the kid a bit, although Ben had been much younger. It was scary to think he was gone, dead. So much for a loving God. That was the trouble with God and church and all that 'Gentle Jesus' stuff, it was all 'be a good boy or go to hell'. There was no fun, just dressing up smart and listening to people rabbit on about the Bible.

Danny led the gang along the road towards the church. It was bitterly cold and they had nowhere to go. It was half past ten.

Geoff and Sarah Notes were fast asleep when the phone rang. It had been a difficult week, and they had gone to bed early feeling drained and exhausted, but also feeling that at last things might have turned a corner. Tragic though the death of young Ben had been, they both sensed that it had been a catalyst for healing relationships within the church.

The urgent tone continued to ring until at last Geoff reached out his hand and grasped the phone to him. 'Hello, Geoff Notes.' His voice was not welcoming. He forced his bleary eyes to focus on the digital clock by the bed, the figures flicked on to 12:43.

'Is that the Reverend Geoffrey Notes, of Redbrook Methodist Church?'

'Yes, to whom am I speaking?'

'Control Room, Redbrook Police Station, sir. There's been an incident at your church, and your attendance at the scene would be appreciated.'

'Incident? What kind of incident?'

'I'm afraid I can't go into details, Reverend,' the

voice sounded officious, 'but a Sergeant Peters is on the scene and will meet you on your arrival.'

Geoff's heart was racing. He had no idea what could possibly necessitate a visit to the church in the middle of the night. He quickly pulled on his jeans, T-shirt and pullover and headed out to the car. Sarah didn't stir, so he decided not to wake her.

He decided it was quicker to walk than to drive, and after a few yards he broke into a run. He cut down an alleyway at the back of the manse and into the street where the church was. As he turned the corner his heart sank.

There were four fire engines with blue lights flashing outside the front of the church. Some five or six police officers were standing beside a white minibus with its protective windscreen grille.

Sergeant Peters stepped out from the cluster of other officers.

'Reverend Notes?'

'Yes, that's me.' Geoff panted breathlessly 'What's happened?'

'Vandals, Mr Notes. That's what's happened. Damn thugs. They've given your place a right good going over. There's a lot of it about.'

Geoff's heart sank. 'Can I see inside?'

The sergeant shrugged his shoulders, as if to imply that he wasn't really bothered, and led Geoff toward the front door of the building. Five large hosepipes snaked their way into the church, and yellow helmeted fire personnel were in the doorway pulling and straightening them. They were preparing to reel them back into the fire appliance.

A team of four fire personnel with 'Investigation Unit' written in bright yellow lettering on their black waterproofs entered the building ahead of Geoff and Sergeant Peters and shone a bright-beamed torch around the blackened interior.

Geoff's eyes followed the beam of the torch. He sighed in disbelief. Graffiti had been spray painted in a complex network of patterns all around the walls.

The 'Investigation Unit' moved toward the seat of the fire—the sanctuary end of the church, which housed the lectern, communion table and font. Geoff and the Sergeant followed on behind. The font was blackened and disfigured, and the ceiling above had disintegrated. Geoff looked up through the blackened beams to the night sky above.

'Looks as if they started the fire here...' said the senior investigator, kneeling beside a pile of ash, 'I reckon they used petrol and newspaper... stupid kids.' The team crowded together and examined the ash, and after several minutes they concluded that a bonfire of hymnbooks and church magazines had been lit beside the font in the corner. The flames had licked up the the wall and set the roof timbers alight.

The ceiling tiles all across the low roofed sanctuary area were hanging down in molten and disfigured shapes. Water was dripping through the gaping hole.

The lectern and communion table were upturned and the cross had been broken in two. Everything was blackened with smoke. Pools of water had gathered on the floor, and the carpet felt sodden underfoot. The stench of burnt plastic and fabric filled the air.

Geoff had seen enough. He courteously bade Ser-

geant Peters goodnight and trudged slowly back
home. He felt very depressed. So much for things
having turned a corner. He had enough problems
on his mind... this was the last straw.

News of the arson at the church spread rapidly
around the community at Redbrook; and everyone
was genuinely shocked that the church had been
vandalised.

Geoff called a meeting of the church council to
survey the damage the following evening. At Geoff's
request Pip had arranged for the scout troop's oil
lamps to be lit around the building so that people
could see. Power would not be restored for three
days.

The Redbrook congregation assembled outside
the front door at 8pm, and after Geoff had warned
them to prepare themselves for the worst, Margaret
unlocked the front door and Pip went inside to light
the lamps.

Miriam followed Geoff and Sarah, her head
wrapped in a beautiful red scarf. She looked drawn
and tired, but she was determined to support the
church in their time of need, as they had supported
her in recent days.

Adam and his wife walked silently hand in hand
looking very upset. Pete, wrapped warmly in a
heavy black top coat, reminded everyone to watch
for the puddles of water across the floor. Bert and
his dog brought up the rear as usual.

The little procession moved slowly and solemnly
around the building, whispering and tutting in disbelief at what they saw. The scene of devastation
was worse than any of them had expected. The
chapel looked a wreck.

At last, after the guided tour was over, Geoff gathered them all at the upturned communion table. With Pete's help he turned it back to its upright position. Geoff picked up the broken wooden cross which was lying in two pieces on the floor, and bound it together with strong red gaffer tape. He placed it lovingly on the communion table.

Sarah stepped forward and pulled open the plastic carrier bag across her arm and pulled out a bottle of wine, a large glass, and a hunk of bread. She placed them gently on the table.

It was a dramatic scene. The flickering lamps. The graffiti ridden sanctuary. The shadowy huddle of worshippers. Yet it was an unforgettable moment for the people of Redbrook Methodist Church. It was, indeed, the moment of renewal... and the moment in which God took this broken congregation and bound it together in the power of His love.

At Geoff's suggestion the church members each prayed before they ate the bread and drank the wine. They were beautiful prayers... prayers of reconciliation, prayers of faith, and prayers of beginning again.

Last of all, as usual, it was Bert's turn to pray and he paused and sighed a deep sigh. 'I see a picture of a broken cross... but now it's back together again.' He smiled a wrinkled smile and took a large hunk of bread and stuffed it in his mouth. Bert's blind eyes hadn't stopped him from seeing what God had done.

There was no interpretation of Bert's vision, for there was no need of one. The tragic divisions within the church at Redbrook had been resolved for ever. Geoff stood and looked at the red binding

and wished that all church crosses could be broken
and re-made this way... as a reminder of the healing grace of Jesus.

The following morning was Saturday. The day of
the great 'clean-up' at Redbrook. The members of
the morning and evening congregations worked
side by side. They painted the walls, they dried the
carpets, they temporarily fixed the low ceiling with
sheets of hardboard... and, although the building
was only a shadow of its former self it was at least
habitable again.

Geoff and Sarah were exhausted by the end of the
day. They strolled home hand-in-hand, aching all
over from the long hours of scrubbing, cleaning and
painting.

'Phew... I'm bushed,' muttered Geoff, as they
opened the front door of the manse and went inside.
Rosie was standing in the hallway, looking radiant.

'Dinner is served,' she beamed, pointing them
toward their own dining room. They opened the
door and saw the table laid exquisitely, complete
with floral display and two candles. 'You just sit
here... tonight, I'm serving you!'

Geoff and Sarah sat down to a four course meal
of soup, steak and three vegetables, fruit salad, and
a selection of cheeses. They sat and ate, and Rosie
served them like an experienced waitress. Even
though they were exhausted, they soon realised how
hungry they were after a day of such heavy work.

As soon as the coffee had been served Rosie
excused herself and disappeared to her room. The
candles were burning low, and Geoff looked across
at his wife in the warm glow of the candlelight and
realised again how much he loved her.

'And are we yet alive... and see each other's face' he whispered, quoting words from an old Methodist hymn.

'Yes, I guess we are, Geoff. Maybe we're even more alive than ever before.'

'When Adam laid hands on me, and I felt God's power filling my life... I was sad that you weren't there to share it with me.'

'I know Geoff, and when you told me about it I was more disappointed than I could ever explain.'

'I'm such a lousy minister to you, Sarah. I rush around caring for everyone else's soul... but your needs are often bottom of the list.'

'I caught you up, tonight, Geoff. As we were praying in the chapel... during the communion... I felt the Holy Spirit flowing over me like a warm shower.'

'And...?'

'It's like I've got everything in balance at last. All our work at Gospel End, it was good, but somehow it was too much in our strength... and not enough in His.'

'Can we start again?'

'How?'

'Be my soul-mate?'

'Yes... if you'll let me.' Sarah smiled and gently blew the candles out. It was the end of an exhausting day.

On Sunday morning at 10 am David signed his discharge papers at Birmingham General, and tore off the plastic identity bracelet which had so irritated him. He walked out into the bright morning sunlight.

He walked slowly through the city, still feeling weak from his beating, and followed the sound of the church bells from St. Martin's in the Bull Ring which rang clearly through the crisp morning air.

As he walked he remembered the events of that dismal night of his mugging, and vowed never to get in such a state again. He looked at his watch, it was opening time. He needed a drink.

He breezed confidently into the pub where he had sat just a few days before, took the same chair at the same table, and drank deeply of the same strong frothy brew. To celebrate his freedom from the hospital and to erase the memory of the taste of the food he ordered a bar meal of steak and chips. He cut through the rather over-done meat and chewed thoughtfully as he reviewed his options. He quite fancied Leeds. It didn't occur to him to think of returning to Pete and Jill in London. He didn't want to be indebted to some middle-class do-gooders, and besides, he was in no mood to face Rosie and the dubious joys of fatherhood. If he dossed down with Pete and Jill they were bound to try to make him face up to his responsibilities. No, Leeds it was. He estimated he could afford another pint. And then another.

Half-way through his third pint he noticed three rough looking men enter the bar and sit at a table near the window. He knew them from somewhere, their faces and voices were familiar, but he couldn't place them.

He peered at them over his pint glass, trying to remember, and as he tried to focus the fuzzy images in his mind he suddenly gasped. Indeed he had seen them before, coming at him with fists and feet in the dark corner of a car park.

Dave was into his fourth pint, and slouched behind a newspaper that had been left by a previous customer, when the taller of the three left the others saying he was 'off for a leak'. As Dave glanced at this tall stranger in his dirty overcoat a hatred welled up within him which felt totally uncontrollable. The man moved clumsily toward the men's toilet and kicked the swing door open, belching loudly as he did so.

In an instant Dave was on his feet and into the men's room. Seconds later he slipped out of the back door of the pub. There was blood on his hands. The knife that he had earlier used to cut his steak was no longer on his plate. He moved swiftly through the back streets and alleyways of the city, snaking his way toward the coach station and glancing behind him for any sight of the other two.

He heard the distant sound of sirens, and felt suddenly afraid. He panicked and started to run, hoping against hope that there might be a coach about to leave. Emerging from an alleyway near the coach station he stopped for a moment to check that it was safe, and then entered, breathless and dishevelled. He desperately scanned the timetable for coaches to Leeds, or to anywhere.

As he stood panting before the sign he became aware of footsteps coming toward him from behind. He turned suddenly and saw a tall policeman approaching. Dave panicked and ran towards the double glass doors of the entry lobby. The policeman, who had been routinely patrolling the bus station and knew nothing of the incident in the pub immediately radioed a description of the fleeing man to central control, before giving chase himself. Dave threw himself through the glass doors and ran full tilt into a group of students who had gathered to see a friend off to London. He tripped over a guitar case and fell forward on to the ground in a spectacular fashion. The policeman was on him before he could regain his feet. 'What's your hurry, son? Miss your bus, did you?' The approaching sound of a police car siren was enough for Dave to realise that it was all over. He looked at his bloody hands and smiled wryly at the policeman.

'It's a fair cop, guv'nor, you got me this time.' He sneered sarcastically.

Geoffrey Notes stood behind the lectern at Redbrook that bright Sunday morning, and grasped it firmly. This was his third sermon to the people of Redbrook, and by far the most important. As he looked out over the familiar faces of people who, only three weeks previously, had been strangers to him, he longed to speak the word of the Lord to them.

'God so loved the world that He gave...' He slowly closed the Bible on the lectern and casually strolled over to the communion table. He picked up the broken cross, and meandered to the front row of his congregation. There was a power and conviction behind each word that made everyone listen.

'The love of God is like the customer at a slave auction, who outbids everyone else in order to set the captive free. God loves us with foolish generosity.

'The love of God is like a debt-collector who

declares the debtor's unpayable account "paid in full". God loves us with foolish generosity.

'The love of God is like the judge who sets the guilty prisoner free, and who pays the fine himself. God loves us with foolish generosity.

'Hosea loved his wife though she was unfaithful, he forgave her when she humiliated him, and bought her back out of slavery. God loves us with a forgiving husband-love like that.

'Isaiah saw love as the love of a mother. Her whole being focused on the delicate new baby, her breasts filling painfully should she ever forget her child. God loves us with a consistent mother-love like that.

'The love of God is like the good shepherd who leaves his flock safe at home to search for the lost lamb in the wilderness. God loves us with a caring shepherd-love like that.

'The love of God is the love of a Father, who, when the guilty son returns broken and defeated, dresses him in a robe, and sets the table for a banquet. God loves us with an accepting father-love like that.

'We have only one mandate for our work, and that is the supreme love of God. There is only one symbol of the church's mission... and it is this... the symbol of the broken cross.'

Geoff paused and turned the cross slowly round in his hand. Every eye was fixed upon it. A long piece of the red tape had come undone, and hung loosely from the cross like a stream of blood.

'The love of God is the love of the cross. What greater love is there than this, that a man lay down his life for his friends?

'None of us have enough love with which to serve the world,' continued Geoff, 'and all of us need to come to the Lord and ask for the empowering of His love for what He calls us to do.

'From now on this church is one family, and it's for all... whether you are rich or poor, simple or intellectual, black or white, radical or charismatic. This is the church where people live their lives together in the suffering love of Jesus and where they share His love for a broken, needy world.'

'Amen. Amen,' shouted Adam.

'Praise the Lord!' shouted Bert.

'Hear, hear,' called Peter, sounding embarrassed.

'And so this morning, after the awful week we've all had... I invite you to come forward to this communion rail and join me here at the broken cross. To receive the love of Jesus, so that you may pass it on to those that need it most.'

Geoff announced the final hymn, his voice wavering with emotion. Sarah smiled lovingly. She still ached for Gospel End, but maybe God was working toward a higher purpose than she had previously understood.

They stood and sang the final hymn...

In Christ there is no east or west,
In Him no south or north;
But one great fellowship of love
Throughout the whole wide earth.

In Him shall true hearts everywhere
Their high communion find;

His service is the golden cord
Close binding all mankind...

By the end of the second verse the communion rail was nearly full, and others were kneeling up the central aisle. Above the chords of the hymn was the sound of weeping.

Adam was kneeling at the centre of the rail, his broad back shaking with emotion. Pete stepped over others in the aisle and carefully picked his way to the front. He squeezed into the last remaining space and placed his arm around Adam's broad bowed shoulders.

'I'm sorry, brother Adam.'

The shoulders shook even more, but there was no reply. Adam was too overcome to speak. Sarah had made her way to Geoff's side by the communion table and they were kneeling, hand-in-hand, as they sang the familiar words.

As the congregation gently sang the closing words of the final verse Sarah felt a body press close to hers. She turned to look at Rosie, whose mascara was running down her cheeks, and squeezed her arm.

'I want in on this stuff...' Rosie brushed her cheek with the back of her hand. 'I never knew He was for real...'

'Welcome to the family,' whispered Sarah, kissing her gently on the cheek.

At this most holy and precious of moments, when a wave of emotion was sweeping over the whole congregation, there was a noise like thunder above. The kids were on the roof again, running to and fro. To them it was just another Sunday.

Geoff stood to give the benediction, and even as he began to say 'The blessing of the...' there was an enormous crash and the temporary boarding which had been carefully erected over the font collapsed in a heap.

The people kneeling at the rail looked up at a dozen faces peering through the gaping hole above.

'What's going on down there?' whispered a ten year old to his older brother.

'It's sort of religious, I think.'

'They look really fed up, don't they? They're all crying.'

'Maybe they're upset about something.'

'Perhaps they don't like the new decorating we did for them,' chuckled a very fat black lad.

One boy backed away from the hole and raced back along the roof, but he knew that it was too late. His father, Adam, had already seen him there.

Geoff stood up and peered through the hole. The other lads began to move away, afraid of what he might do. 'I'll give a quid to every lad who can jump from up there onto this communion table... without hurting himself.' He dragged the shiny communion table until it was directly below the hole some five feet above.

There was a tense moment of indecision, then one boy after another made the perilous leap from 'up there' to 'down here', and Geoff dished out gold coins from the offering bowl to each of them in turn. The penitent congregation was wide-eyed in amazement. Some of them clearly disapproved.

When the last of the lads had descended and the penitents at the rail had all stood up and returned to their seats... Geoffrey Notes held up the broken cross.

'This is just a simple announcement, to say that the 'Broken Cross' gang, to be known as the 'BC's, will meet here on Fridays from this week. It's going to be the greatest gang Redbrook has ever seen.'

God had shown them who needed His love the most.

Chapter Eleven

It was nearly 2 pm by the time that Geoff, Sarah and Rosie arrived back at the manse after that eventful Sunday service. They were all feeling very hungry and set about making a quick mixed grill.

There was much to talk about. The response to Geoff's sermon, the hole in the roof, and the unexpected launch of the BC gang. The three of them were chatting happily in the kitchen when there was a loud knock at the door. Sarah grimaced. 'Who on earth...?'

'I'll go' said Geoff kindly, 'I'll be back in a minute.'

He opened the heavy front door and found Adam standing there with Danny by his side. The young man looked decidedly uncomfortable.

'Come in,' smiled Geoff, 'it's good to see you.'

The three of them stepped into the front room. 'This is my son, Daniel... and I think he has something to say to you, Pastor.'

Adam and his son sat on the sofa, with Geoff on

the easy chair facing them. 'Yes?' Geoff looked questioningly.

'I'm sorry,' the lad muttered in a barely audible whisper.

'Louder, son, louder,' boomed Adam.

The boy looked up at his father with eyes which asked 'must I?' Adam looked stern.

'I'm sorry, pastor.' It was much louder this time.

'Sorry for what?' smiled Geoff.

'Sorry that we broke up your church the other night. It started off as a laugh... we didn't mean to do so much damage. Honest.'

'What's done is done,' Geoff responded warmly, 'It's the future that counts. Are you going to help me with the BC gang?'

The teenager relaxed. He'd expected the minister to bawl at him... not ask him to join a youth club. 'What d'you need?' he inquired unenthusiastically.

'You... and your mates... and I need advice on what kind of things you guys like to do. Could a couple of you come round here tomorrow night at eight?'

An evening with the vicar was not Danny's idea of a good time but it might make life easier at home if he was seen to be cooperating. Parents liked that kind of thing. Besides his father had decreed that Danny was not to be allowed out of the flat for any reason other than for school for at least the next month. Even an evening with the vicar was better than an evening with his twin sisters.

'Okay.' Danny shrugged his shoulders, as if in agreement, then looked up at his father as if asking permission to leave. Adam nodded in agreement and Danny quickly left.

'I've also come to say sorry,' Adam drawled in his deep voice.

'You weren't with the vandals, too, were you Adam?' Geoff smiled, but Adam seemed unimpressed. 'Oh no, not that. I'm sorry because I've been trying to push the Rainbow Arch ministry team onto you... and everyone else.'

'That's okay, Adam, you are entitled to your view of things.'

'Let me finish, pastor... I wasn't doing it in the right spirit. I wasn't asking the Lord what He wanted... I was just pushing my own thing.'

'What's changed your mind?' Geoff had rather liked the idea of some preparatory training all expenses paid in Texas. He could see it about to evaporate before him.

'Danny. Danny's changed my mind. I was looking to the Rainbow Arch team to sweep in and change the world... painlessly, easily, cleanly... and preferably within a fortnight. I thought that somehow they'd sort everything out. Even Danny.'

Geoff leant forward intently. 'And won't they?'

'When I saw his face up on the roof this morning I realised that no American Crusade would bring him in. They're a million miles from where he's at. No, he needs someone to get close to him, to care long term.'

'That's what mission is, Adam. It's being where the people are, and bringing the living Jesus there. It's costly, and sometimes it's very painful.' Mentally Geoff waved goodbye to Texas. Somehow he felt it didn't matter, the tanned and no doubt charismatic Doctor Nodder would serve God elsewhere. It was he, Geoff Notes, who had been called to serve

Redbrook. As he looked at Adam's creased and worried face he felt a calmness and certainty that all things were working to good.

'You can count on me, pastor. Anything you need... I'm your main man.'

'It's a fine son you've got there, Adam, how old is he?'

'Thirteen years... but he's been running wild on the estate. I can't seem to tame him any more. I need your help, Geoff.'

Geoff chuckled. 'I'm not into taming people... I'm into making them wild for the Lord!'

'Hallelujah' beamed Adam, 'I guess that's what they pay you for!'

He glanced at his chunky gold braceleted watch. 'I must go. The kids are in the car outside. We're off visiting family.'

Geoff opened the front door and watched Adam climb into his shiny old Ford Cortina packed full of children. He started the engine and a puff of exhaust filled the air. With a smile and a wave, he was gone.

Geoff closed the front door and went back to the kitchen. Sarah and Rosie had finished eating their mixed grill and were so engrossed in conversation that they didn't even turn when Geoff entered the room. He quietly took his meal from under the grill and sat at the table beside Sarah.

'I really did want a baby, you know... I didn't really care whose it was, as long as I got one.'

'Why did you want a baby, Rosie, why so much?' Sarah was watching Rosie intently.

'For the love. I mean, babies bring love into your

life. I've never had much luck with men. But a baby, that's different. They make you feel secure.'

Sarah looked concerned. 'Rosie, I'm so pleased you've not had an abortion... that you've decided to keep it... but now that you've become a Christian...'

Geoff turned and looked at his wife in surprise. 'A Christian...?'

Sarah cut his sentence short with a sharp look. 'Now that you've become a Christian Jesus is your security. He's the one to bring love into your life. From now on life's about what you can give to the baby... not what the baby can give to you.'

'Love, you mean?'

'Yes. Just when we think we've run out of the stuff we can go back to Him for more. That's why we invited you to stay here.'

'And why Pete's forgiven Dave?'

'Yes.'

'And that's why we're starting the BC club for the kids who vandalised the church,' whispered Geoff, thoughtfully.

'And that's why Margaret Briggs has invited you and the baby to go and live at her place, for as long as you want. She says her house is too big... and she's always wanted kids around the place.'

Rosie's eyes opened wide in amazement.

The knocker on the front door sounded again, there was an urgency in the beat. Sarah sighed, 'No peace for the wicked,' and went to open it.

Pete strolled in wearing a smart leather car-coat and kid gloves. He looked upset. 'Is the boss home?'

Sarah showed him into the kitchen, and Pete

pulled up the fourth chair at the kitchen table. Geoff was still tucking into his mixed grill.

'Bad news, folks.' Pete looked deadly serious.

Geoff put down his knife and fork. 'Is it Dave?'

'Got it in one, my friend. He was on his way to the coach station in Birmingham when he saw the three men who mugged him. I'm afraid he... he did something stupid.'

Tears were welling in Rosie's eyes. 'Did what?...'

'He stabbed one of them. The man's in the General. It's touch and go. Dave's in police custody. I think he'll find it difficult to get off this time. It's such a stupid waste.'

Tears fell down Rosie's cheeks. 'I thought he was getting sorted out. How could he have been so stupid? He never bloody thinks, he don't.'

'Anyway, I must be on my way, I want to be there before dark.'

'Where?' asked Sarah inquisitively.

'Birmingham. I've booked into a hotel. The custody officer says that I can see Dave briefly tonight, and I'm seeing Dave's solicitor first thing in the morning. I figure that Dave's going to need all the help he can get.'

Geoff looked at Pete in admiration. 'Thanks, Pete. I'm really grateful.'

Pete looked across at Geoff. 'You... you're grateful? No, it's me... I'm grateful. I've learnt so much about the Lord since you guys came. It's not all words, it's about receiving and it's about giving...'

Geoff looked at Pete and loved him like a brother. He knew that God was changing him from a debater into a doer. 'We'll pray for you, Pete.'

Pete got up to leave. Rosie's eyes were red with tears. 'Give him my love...'

Sarah got up to show Pete to the door. She opened it and smiled warmly as he went towards his car. 'By the way,' she called, 'I really like the new haircut.'

Pete left his hotel in Birmingham soon after 9 am on Monday morning and made his way to the solicitor's office in a back-street behind the city centre police station. It was quite the crummiest solicitor's practice he'd ever seen.

Mr. French had been the duty solicitor on call the previous day when Dave had been arrested and, having a practice built solidly on Legal Aid clients, he had readily agreed to take on Dave's case. As Pete looked at the peeling paintwork and decaying frontage he wondered if he should hire someone else to look after Dave's interests.

Pete was welcomed by the receptionist and shown into a smart office full of shelves of important-looking legal books. Mr French, the solicitor, was seated behind the desk. He was a smartly dressed young man in an immaculate pin-striped suit. He didn't look anything like Pete had imagined him.

'Ah. Mr Peter Bramwell? Come in. You're here in connection with young David Wilson. Yes?'

'Yes.' Pete felt awkward—out of his depth.

'What's your interest in this case? Are you a relative?'

'No. No I'm just a sort of... friend.'

Mr French looked at him quizzically. 'Sort of?'

'I know him through the church. We've been

trying to help.' Pete felt embarrassed at his explanation. It sounded as if he was some kind of do-gooder, but it wasn't like that at all.

'It doesn't look good, you know. The injuries are severe, and it's still possible that the victim might die.'

'I know.'

'Why are you bothered?' The solicitor sounded softer, he was genuinely interested.

'Because Dave's a person... and he's had a lot of bad breaks in his life. I want to help restore the balance.'

'Join the club,' smiled Mr French.

'What do you mean?' Pete looked puzzled.

'That's why I'm here, doing this, instead of carving out myself a nice little earner in litigation like any sensible lawyer.' He leant back in his swivel chair, his hands behind his head. 'Just think, if I hadn't been dragged to a Billy Graham rally a few years back I could have been a rich man by now.'

'And what about Dave... can you get him off?'

'I doubt that very much. But maybe I can make sure he gets a fair deal... and that he's treated like a human being.'

'Don't you ever get disillusioned? Dealing with people like Dave all the time?'

'Yes. Nearly every day.' The lawyer smiled warmly.

'Why go on, then?' Pete was genuinely interested.

'Because that's the job we've all been called to do.'

'What job's that?'

'Redemption, Mr Bramwell. The slow painstaking work of redemption.'

Coffee arrived, and the two men talked on, sharing moments of Christian reality amid the pressures of a busy Monday morning. It was a conversation which would set Peter Bramwell on the first steps to becoming a probation officer.

Promptly at eight o'clock that same Monday evening the manse door-knocker thudded loudly, announcing the arrival of the 'BC' gang. Geoff opened the door and saw eight lads and one girl standing there. They were a motley crew, with their baseball caps, torn jeans and brightly coloured fashion jackets.

'Come in... come in.' He pointed them toward the lounge. 'I'll just get some cans of coke out of the fridge.' He hoped he had enough, he hadn't expected quite such a large deputation.

The group sat around the lounge of the manse, somewhat overawed by the middle class surroundings. They were whispering to one another, as if in a holy place.

Geoff returned with the cokes and handed them round, then sat on the floor, his back against the wall.

'Thanks for coming guys. I really want to get to know you all, and so does everyone at church. The question is, if we start a club, what kind of club do you want?'

Silence. The kids looked down at their feet as if in embarrassment... all except for Adam's son, Danny.

'We'll not come if it's boring. It's not going to be

religious, is it?' He said 'religious' as if it were an offensive word.

'Oh no, no, not services or anything like that…'

'What then?' Danny snapped.

'You tell me, guys. Well, let me give you a few ideas, see how you feel?'

Danny was obviously the spokesman and unofficial leader of the group, because whatever he said was echoed by murmurs of approval from the rest of the gang.

'How about a club with table tennis, games… that sort of stuff?' Geoff could see from their expressions that they didn't think much of the idea.

'There's one of them at the community centre already. No-one goes.' There was a note of finality in the girl's voice. She blew a large pink bubble which Geoff nervously watched grow and then pop. He suddenly felt concerned for the safety of his furniture.

'Or a youth fellowship? You could come round here on Sundays and we could talk about life… stuff you're interested in.'

'Boring'. Danny snapped. The others murmured agreement.

'Perhaps we could build canoes—and then learn how to use them?'

Danny sighed. 'Sounds like school.'

Geoff was beginning to feel frustrated. It seemed that there was no way of pleasing them. 'Well, how about you lot doing something for other people. Sort of community service… visiting old people, doing their gardens, stuff like that.'

Danny yawned, and a couple of the others yawned in sympathy.

Just then Geoff noticed the top of a can of spray paint peeking out of Danny's jacket. He had a flash of inspiration.

'Well, you lot have made a right mess of this estate, haven't you? You've sprayed your paint over every wall in sight, every lift in the flats, and all over the inside of my church.'

Danny smirked. 'The place needed brightening up a bit, didn't it lads?' They all agreed, including the girl.

'Well if you wanted to brighten the place up... you might at least have made a good job of it.'

'Like what?' Danny looked annoyed.

'Made pictures instead of insane scribbles that any kid in the playgroup could have done.'

'That's modern art, that is,' retorted Danny.

'It's just a mess, and you know it is. But you lot can do better...much better...really make Redbrook look good.'

The enthusiasm in Geoff's voice was infectious, and they were leaning forward. He had struck a rich seam of interest, and he knew it.

'You know the wall at the side of the church... the one that faces the rec. and the flats?'

'Yes,' they replied in unison.

'Boring, isn't it? Just a dirty brown wall.'

'Yes,' they replied again.

'I'd like to give it to you... to do something with. I'm sure the church members won't mind. You can have it on one condition...'

'What's that?' Danny was spokesman again.

'That you'll let us work on it with you, so that it's a real community effort. We've even got a girl at church who's been to art college, I'm sure she'll help us do it right.'

Danny looked round the rest of his gang, as if collecting votes. 'It's a deal. Give us some skin.' He held out his hand and Geoff slapped it. And so Redbrook community mural was born.

Chapter Twelve

The process of preparing for the mural was more complicated than Geoff had imagined. To his great delight the church council readily agreed to the idea, especially when he explained that this was just the first of many projects which he hoped that the 'BC' gang might tackle.

'What I like most about this concept,' he explained enthusiastically, 'is that it'll give many of us the chance to get to know these kids on a one-to-one basis. I feel strongly that what they all lack is a range of real relationships with grown-ups who care.'

The borough planning officer needed more persuasion, however. It seemed that Geoff's ministry constantly brought him into conflict with planning officers. He felt that a highly coloured wall might throw the 'carefully designed features around the recreation ground out of balance'. After nearly forty-five minutes of talking round in circles Geoff somewhat uncharacteristically lost his temper.

'Carefully designed features?' he shouted. 'I've seen more imaginative car parks. The place is a mess. If you make people live in a mess, they'll treat it like one. Those kids are going to paint somewhere and so it may as well be on a wall where the paint is wanted.' The planning officer, who was not used to people shouting at him, was hurt.

At the second meeting with the planning officer Geoff took Sergeant Peters from Redbrook police station along with him. The sergeant's evidence was convincing.

'If we can get these kids to paint that wall instead of every other wall on the estate... it will be a major victory,' the sergeant explained. He admired Geoff's positive response to the vandalism he'd experienced in the church, and felt that any community response to the problem could only be positive.

The planning officer, who was deeply embarrassed by the vandalised appearance of what had once been his 'showpiece overspill estate', conceded defeat and reluctantly tendered his support.

There was no shortage of volunteers from members of the church. Pip was ecstatic about the concept, and Adam thought that it might just 'do the trick for Danny'. Miriam stood in her prophetic pose again and challenged them all by asking if there would be any prayer backing for the mural.

'Since we all started praying together this church has changed. It's changed a lot. Well, we haven't been meeting in the mornings since Ben died, and I think it's time we started again. If we're going to reach these kids we're going to need the power of the Holy Spirit to help us do it.'

Pete seconded the proposal. 'If there's one thing I've learnt since Geoff came, it's that prayer is what connects things together. I'm willing to come here one morning a week to pray for the kids. Will anyone join me?'

There was a chorus of 'Amen's and 'I'll be there's, and Geoff gazed out at his united flock in wonder and pride. He knew that a church bound together in prayer and service could really go places fast.

Bert, who appeared slightly embarrassed about the whole thing, quietly approached Geoff at the end of the meeting with his faithful guide-dog by his side. He was his usual gracious self. 'Well, Geoff, this is one project where I can't be of much help. My eyes being what they are.'

'I'm sorry, Bert,' Geoff groaned in embarrassment, 'I never thought, I really didn't do it to exclude you.'

'Oh Geoff, don't be silly... I never thought you did! But I was wondering... do you mind if I do the brushes?'

'The brushes?' Geoff asked. 'What about the brushes?'

Bert scratched his chin. 'Well, I've got a bit of money put by, and I'd like to buy the brushes. I expect you'll need a lot, with all these kids involved!'

Geoff smiled. 'Thanks Bert, that's very...'

'Just a minute,' Bert continued, 'but I'd also like to look after them. Wash them, take care of them... so that there'll always be a big bucketful ready to choose from.'

'Thanks, Bert, you're a saint.'

'And I'll be praying over the brushes...' Geoff looked at him, puzzled, not really understanding what he meant.

Bert was as good as his word, and all through the mural project he attended every planning meeting and every group discussion and sat quietly whilst they tried out their designs on rolls of scrap wallpaper.

They used Bert as a sounding board for their ideas, and in having to describe their efforts to him, they often saw the weakness of their design. Bert's gentle and encouraging comments helped them to glimpse a vision of what could be. And when work started on the wall itself Bert sat on a chair beside them, washing the brushes and urging them on. And, all the time, Bert prayed.

Pip was appointed senior designer and voluntary 'artist in residence'. To her it was a dream come true. Her three years at art college had been followed by a long period of unemployment and disillusionment. She had been unable to find any job even vaguely connected with art. For the last two years she had been 'filling in' as a check-out assistant in a local supermarket.

The wall was divided into sections, and different members of the church were allocated areas to work on with various members of the BC gang. After a lot of discussion and experimentation everyone agreed that the mural should reflect London life, and each team adopted its own individual style and theme. The mural was to become a multi-faceted jig-saw which was linked together in jagged and irregular ways... rather like life itself.

Margaret's little group decided to depict the

heart of London, for the people of Redbrook really considered themselves Londoners. Her piece of the jigsaw was the 'skyline' at the top of the mural, which would set the rest in context.

She took five kids up to Victoria Street after school one day and introduced them to all her old colleagues at work. She felt very proud of her rowdy group of street-kids, who seemed so out of context in the formal offices of the D.T.I.

Mabel, her former secretary, seemed quite shocked when she referred to the kids as 'my gang' and only just suppressed laughter when she realised that they all referred to her as 'Duchess'.

Her old boss wasn't too impressed when she stood them, one by one, onto her old desk to look out of the window. Then, finally, she clambered up herself to take one last view of Big Ben and West-minster Abbey, the view that had been so much a part of her previous life. From her vantage point on the desk she could see more of the Abbey and the Palace of Westminster than she had ever been able to see before. She sighed a sigh of regret. And then it suddenly dawned on her how she must look to her staid former colleagues as she precariously bal-anced there. Margaret Briggs started to laugh. She laughed at the absurdity of her position and at the looks on their faces. She was seeing more than she had ever seen before because she was stood on a desk with a group of kids rather than sat behind it shuffling bits of paper. In all the years she worked in the Civil Service she had never once stood on a desk and taken in the view. She had been content to stay on the floor and make do with a more restricted outlook. Maybe she was nearer the heart of things now than she'd ever been. With great dignity Margaret climbed down and thanked her former colleagues and the fresh faced youngster who had taken over her desk. Then she turned to her charges and said 'Race you to the lift; last one there buys beefburgers for everyone.'

She bought them all burgers and chips at a fast-food restaurant in Victoria Street. The server gave them all free cardboard crowns to wear, so they put them on and celebrated like royalty at a feast; and they all laughed a lot.

Rosie hosted a group on 'motherhood', and Sarah went along to give her moral support. Sarah was disappointed that no boys wanted to join the group, but took it as another indicator of 'sexism within the education system'.

Four girls joined them on the trip to a special baby unit run by a Roman Catholic Order for 'unwanted babies awaiting adoption'. The nuns, who didn't wear habits or observe strict rules about silence, made them very welcome. A cheerful 'mother superior' type lady taught them about the realities of parenting. They entered a gaily coloured nursery with pictures on the wall and mobiles hanging from the ceiling. Each child had its own cot and its name was written in brightly coloured felt-tip ink on a sign attached to one end. Several of the babies were crying. They weren't hungry, it was explained, they needed changing. It was a 'live' demonstration, and not particularly pleasant to watch—or smell!

Then each of the girls was given a baby to hold. Patiently, and under the sharp oversight of a friendly novice, they each experienced the intangible relationship which develops when you feed a small baby its bottle.

It was excellent practice for Rosie, who, being seven months pregnant, was looking much bigger than her usual slim self. She gently lifted the bottle to the baby's lips and looked down at the little face looking trustingly up at her. She was thankful to God, and thankful to Margaret Briggs that her own baby would be born with the security of a home of its own. She swore silently that her baby would never suffer the neglect and abuses that she had.

As Sarah stood and watched Rosie feeding the new baby she was mesmerized. As she looked at Rosie's swollen shape she felt a tinge of jealousy and, for the first time in her life, she wondered if motherhood might figure in her own future plans.

Pip used a borrowed scout minibus to take her group to a nature reserve in Surrey. There they saw protected species of birds and animals living free in a very overgrown environment. A long-haired conservationist dressed like a hippie held them spellbound as she talked about dodos, whales and ozone. She also taught them about the urban wildlife that they could look out for themselves. Even kestrels and foxes could be spotted in Redbrook if they knew where to look and were patient. Pip began to dream of an inner city wildlife sanctuary supported by the church and the community. Later she would share these ideas with Jill and they would both start the long search for a suitable site.

They cooked 'dampers and twists' over an open fire in good scouting tradition and, before they left, were taken into the barn to see a new baby fawn which the 'hippie lady' had recently rescued.

Pip knelt in the hay and held out a dish of warm milk to the fawn. She whispered softly, coaxing the baby deer to come to her. The children watched in wonder as the fawn stood and listened, as if wondering if it could trust the stranger. Then, quite suddenly, it moved slowly and unsteadily on long bandy legs toward her. It not only licked all of the milk out of the bowl... it licked Pip's hand, as well.

Adam's group went to an exhibition of Caribbean culture at the Commonwealth Institute, and several of them were invited to play on oil drums with a West Indian band. They went back to Adam's place for a huge plate of rice and peas, and he told them a gripping story about slavery and the price of freedom. Then they watched a video about the beaches of the Caribbean, and Adam explained how he hadn't been able to find a job in years.

Sarah, supported by Rosie, took her group to Waterloo after school one Friday. Rosie showed them the patch of pavement in the underpass where she used to sleep. She told them about the squat, about the hard times she'd known... and about Dave. She spoke without passion, in almost a monotone, but those who heard her lost any notions about running away to 'the bright lights of the city' forever. They began to realise how desperate a person had to be before enduring the indignity and hardships of living rough. Several of the kids in the group who had thought it might be fun were profoundly shocked by what they heard and saw.

Afterwards they went to a large Victorian-looking church nearby and were welcomed by the minister who gave them hot cross buns and orange squash. After tea they stood behind a table at what looked like the biggest jumble sale in the world and watched the big doors of the main hall swing open.

Dozens of people from 'cardboard city' streamed in. The clothes which had been spread so neatly over the trestle tables were soon wrenched and pulled in all directions. Right there, without any changing cubicles, people were trying on trousers, skirts and shoes.

Miriam took some of the kids to the intensive care ward where Ben had died, and the staff gave them coke and crisps. They met the doctors who had treated Ben, and heard about his unsuccessful struggle for life. As a special treat they got to look through a viewing window into an operating theatre.

The visit proved to be a deep healing experience for Miriam. It was the first time she'd been back to the hospital since Ben's death, and she was able to thank the staff for their help and support... especially the South African sister, who'd shown a special interest in Ben, and who'd attended his funeral.

Just before they left Miriam took them into the empty cubicle where Ben had died and she told them all about the son she'd loved and lost. It was a very moving moment.

Pete and Jill arranged for the three members of their group to visit Dave in a prison in Kent. It wouldn't have been possible without the help of a very supportive prison chaplain, who had been spending a lot of time with Dave.

The prison chaplain welcomed them at the

prison gate and made a great fuss of them all. He had gained the governor's permission to take them on a tour of the prison, and it proved to be a very disturbing experience for two of the lads in the group who'd already been up before the Juvenile Court.

They met Dave in the 'Visiting Room', a very dingy place which stank of cigarette smoke. He told them about what it was like to be on remand, awaiting trial for murder. If he was found guilty he would be sentenced to life imprisonment. Dave had been inside before but never for anything remotely as serious as murder. He had lost a lot of the arrogance and cynicism that had characterised his life up to his arrest. The last couple of months had given him time to reflect. He told the group how much he valued his friendship with Pete, Jill, and Rosie. And for the first time Pete and Jill believed him. They had been praying for Dave to come to know the Lord. (They would have been disappointed to know that he was using the pages of the Bible they had given him to roll his own cigarettes.)

Geoff's group was the smallest. In fact, only one person opted to join the 'Christian topic' team and that was Danny. Even he hadn't joined because of the religious title, but because he figured that Geoff was an 'okay' sort of bloke and because his father still mentioned the vandalised church now and then.

Geoff took him to Wesley's chapel, and tried to explain about the history of Methodism. He had hoped that the centrepiece of the mural might be a picture of John Wesley riding on his horse through

Redbrook. Danny, however, was singularly unimpressed. Geoff only rescued the day from disaster by taking Danny on to a sci-fi movie presentation in Leicester Square.

On the train back home Geoff tried once again to spark Danny's imagination with the 'horse' concept... but Danny was too engrossed with the grotesque alien monsters and shining metallic automatons to show any interest. The stunning visual effects of galaxies, planets and strange coloured suns had made a great impression on the young lads imagination.

Danny went home with Geoff for supper, and they sat in the kitchen drinking frothy hot chocolate and discussing the 'grossest movies they'd ever seen'.

Sarah broke into Danny's particularly gruesome story about decapitation as she yelled from upstairs. 'Hey guys... I'm up in the attic. Can I have some help?' Geoff and Danny climbed the stairs and looked up into the loft at Sarah's dirty face and her long dark hair hanging down toward them.

'I've found something you'd lost, Geoff... here, let me hand it down.' She lowered a package wrapped in a black plastic bin liner, and Geoff reached up to grasp it.

'What on earth...?' He unravelled the plastic, '...well I'm blowed.'

It was the dart-board that he'd had from being a kid. It had been presented to him by his old youth club leader, the bank manager, when he had left his home church to go to train for the ministry.

Geoff hurried downstairs clutching the dartboard

under his arm. He ran into the study, opened his desk and pulled out the black case which contained his three favourite darts.

He set up the board above his desk and took aim. Danny looked up at him, admiringly, he was quite the maddest vicar that he'd ever met. Geoff froze, turned to Danny, and handed over the dart. 'Your throw first, young man.'

Geoff smiled as he watched Danny's uncertain throw. Over the next couple of hours Geoff told Danny everything he knew about darts. Game followed game, and as they played, Geoff explained how once he'd been a street kid too... and how the church youth club had changed his life. His love of darts had led to his love of the Lord. The numerous tiny holes in the wall surrounding the dartboard were a small price to pay for the light of genuine enthusiasm in Danny's eyes.

The painting of the Redbrook mural stretched over most weekends from March until May. It was by no means easy to hold such a diverse group of people together. Several church members who had been totally behind the scheme in theory found that in practice it took up too much of their valuable spare time. They began to make excuses for not attending the work sessions, and some of them even questioned the validity of the project on the grounds that it was not overtly spreading the gospel.

'We should be preaching the good news to these youngsters, not indulging them by letting them deface our wall.'

Geoff would patiently explain to this minority that some of the BC gang were coming into the church for the occasional service of their own free will. And that he sometimes had as many as seventeen round at the manse on a Friday evening for hot drinks and biscuits, and that the conversations often led to God and Jesus.

Geoff found that a genuine interest in Christian matters arose naturally, so long as he didn't try to force the subject. He was also discovering that a good many of the parents, especially those of the younger children, were appreciative of the interest the church was taking in their sons and daughters. Anything that kept them off the streets and out of danger was accepted as a good thing once it was clear that Geoff and the church members weren't trying to brainwash anyone. Methodism, apparently, was deemed harmless.

The biggest problems came from the young people themselves. At the start of the project over thirty had been involved, but over the weeks many just drifted away. Some of the local children who had left the project or who had never belonged started trying to make life difficult for those who stuck with it. A good deal of teasing was endured about being 'religious nuts' and 'Bible bashers'. Strangely, the effect of this on those who were committed to the gang was to make them more determined to see the project through. They endured the insults and to them it became a matter of pride to be a member of the BC gang. You had to be 'tough' to belong.

The teasing gradually turned nastier. One night the mural, then half completed, was vandalised. Geoff found out what had happened as he passed by the church the next morning. Obscenities were sprayed over a large area of the work. Blue aerosol paint dripped over lovingly painted scenes. It was as though some of the kids were tempting the church to pack it in and to go back inside the four walls of their cosy little sanctuary.

That evening a group from the church met to assess the ruined picture and to decide what to do about it. Pip was devastated and many of those who had committed a lot of time and effort began to wonder if it was all worth while. It was Geoff's granite-like resolve and undiminished enthusiasm which re-lit the flame of hope among them.

The next evening Danny showed up on Geoff and Sarah's doorstep. Sarah ushered him into the living room, and Geoff turned the television off. Geoff stared in amazement at the state of Danny's face. His bottom lip was swollen and bleeding and his left eye was partially closed due to swelling.

'What happened?' demanded Sarah, who was ready to call the police. Danny smiled as best he could.

'I fixed it,' he said.

'Fixed what?'

'Them what done the mural, they won't do it again. I fixed it.' Danny obviously felt some pride in his achievement.

'Don't tell me you had a fight over the mural?' groaned Geoff.

'They shouldn't have done what they done.' This was a statement of fact, not an excuse. 'You said we have to fight for what we believe in like what them first Christians did.'

Geoff remembered telling the Gang about the early church martyrs a few weeks previously. He had told them in gripping and gory detail all about persecution in order to show the kids that you didn't have to be a wimp to be a Christian. Evidently Danny had gotten hold of the wrong end of the stick. 'The early martyrs didn't go beating up their Roman persecutors, Danny.'

Danny tried to grin and failed. 'Yeah, but them Romans were nice compared to the kids round here. I had to get some respect before I could turn the other cheek, like.'

Geoff sighed. He didn't know whether to be angry or proud at this young man's defence of the honour of the BC gang and the church. 'Danny,' he said. 'Christians don't beat people up just because they do something bad.'

'I know, but I ain't a Christian. Not yet at least.'

Sarah left the two talking and went to 'phone Adam and tell him that Danny was going to be spending the night at their place. She felt it would be better for Danny if his mother and father didn't see him until the worst of the bruising went down. She explained to Adam that his son was having a deep spiritual conversation with Geoff and that it might be wise to leave them to it. Adam was delighted.

Eventually, despite the ups and downs, the mural was finished. It was to be unveiled on May 24th, Wesley Day, and Geoff managed to arrange for the President of the Methodist Conference to perform the great ceremony. Geoff borrowed tarpaulins from a local haulage contractor and, once the mural was complete, they were suspended over the wall so that the moment of 'opening' would have the greatest impact.

On May 24th the whole community gathered for the great unveiling. The mayor, the planning officer, the police superintendent, the member of parliament, and many other local dignitaries showed up. They were all grateful to Geoff that the spray painting around the estate had significantly decreased since the launch of the mural project. The council had even been able to clean up some of the concrete walls and Redbrook wasn't looking quite as much a prime example of urban decay as once it had been.

The Salvation Army band stood on the green in front of the tarpaulins playing hymns that bright warm May evening. Then, at a given signal by Geoff Notes, they marched to one side. The dignitaries processed onto the field and were seated on a raised platform to the right of the mural. A large crowd stood on the rec. in front of the tarpaulin covers and waited in anticipation. They all knew what the mural looked like, they had seen its development week by week, but there was something special about an unveiling. Many were there simply to say thank you to those who had put so much effort in on their behalf.

After several rather tedious speeches by local community leaders the President of the Conference stepped forward to the microphone to perform the great unveiling ceremony.

'I name this mural 'Broken Cross' and pronounce it officially unveiled' he declared, looking very solemn in his long black cassock. The tarpaulin collapsed to the ground in a crumpled heap.

Everyone applauded loudly, and gazed in admiration at the many pictures within the jig-saw of shapes. They 'oohed' at the beautiful skyline of London and 'aahed' at the panoply of pictures which colourfully filled the wall.

'I am very glad to be here today, and I bring you the greetings of the whole church. Your Minister tells me that the mural you see before you is about Christ's love for us, and our love for the world. And now, a reading from Scripture...

'Matthew's Gospel, chapter 25 and verse 34:

'Then the King will say to the people on his right, "Come you that are blessed by my Father! Come and possess the Kingdom which has been prepared for you ever since the creation of the world."

(The president, as Geoff had instructed him, looked up at the top of the picture and saw a lot of people wearing crowns marching down Victoria Street).

'I was hungry and you fed me,' (he paused dramatically and looked at the picture of the 'unwanted baby' unit and the young novice, who strongly resembled Sarah in the picture).

'Thirsty and you gave me a drink,' (the president peered at a whole host of near extinct animals which were eating out of a woman's hand.)

'I was a stranger and you received me,' (he looked quizzically at a picture of Adam stepping out of a Caribbean beach scene and into the flats at Redbrook), 'Naked and you clothed me,' (he adjusted his spectacles and peered at what appeared to be a fight at a jumble sale).

'I was sick, and you took care of me,' (There was the South African ward sister standing beside Ben, who was looking radiantly fit and well, in the intensive care ward.)

'In prison and you visited me.' (Everyone looked at Dave, sitting in his cell and talking to the prison chaplain).

People applauded. The President smiled and shook Geoff warmly by the hand, and forgetting that the amplifier was still turned on he continued: 'Well done, Geoffrey. You've done a good job. But what's that in the middle of the picture?'

'Oh that... it's my handiwork... together with Danny, sir. It's a picture of the galaxy, and in the middle there's a dartboard... with a broken cross stuck in the bull's-eye. Oh yes, and the cross is stuck together with red sticky tape.'

'Oh... I see...' murmured the president, but he didn't. He'd have preferred a picture of John Wesley riding through Redbrook on his horse.

Geoff turned to the waiting audience. 'Tea and jam doughnuts are now being served in the newly re-decorated church hall. Today they're 'on the house'... do come inside and have a doughnut on us!'

Geoff smiled at the President, who was still trying to grasp the religious significance of Geoff's handiwork. How could he begin to explain that the symbol of the galaxy, the dartboard and the broken cross was not only the centrepiece of the Redbrook mural but the centrepiece of his life?

Epilogue

Less than a month after the unveiling of the
Redbrook mural Pete hired a fifty-two seater luxury
coach for the church outing to Nottingham. It came
equipped with video and television screens, toilet
and washroom, air-conditioning, and a hostess who
made hot drinks in a kitchen at the rear.

But this was no ordinary outing. Some forty
people from Redbrook were going to Nottingham to
witness the ordination of Geoffrey Notes, their 'pro-
bationer' minister. None of them had been to an
ordination before, and there was a real buzz of
excitement as they imagined what it might be like.

'Where is Geoff, I thought it was his big day?'
Rosie asked Margaret Briggs, as she looked around
the coach for Geoff or Sarah.

'He's gone up there with Sarah already. He's got
to meet the President and other dignitaries.' Margaret smiled.

'What is an ordination, anyway?' Rosie asked, as
Margaret nursed the new baby.

'It's a time when a minister makes promises to God. Like getting married, but to the church.'

'But I thought he was a minister already.' Rosie evidently thought that 'ordinations' were stupid.

'No, up to now Geoff's been on probation.' Margaret cuddled the baby and 'cooed' at it.

'On probation...' Rosie laughed. 'Sounds like he's been a naughty boy!'

The luxury 'Executive-liner' pulled in to the coach park outside the city's main concert hall, where the ordination was to be held. There were lines of coaches from all over the country, each unloading their smartly dressed passengers. Thirty ministers were to be ordained at this huge ceremony, and people had come from far and wide to support their candidate.

The driver reversed the coach smoothly into the allotted bay and turned off the engine. The next coach to arrive reversed into the space alongside, but it looked shabby in contrast. Pete remarked to the driver that it resembled a museum piece. Its rugged appearance and hard plastic seats fitted the company's name admirably... 'The Economy Bus and Coach Company. Great Orton.'

The passengers from both coaches disembarked and intermingled as they were ushered into the beautiful concert hall. There was a loud buzz of conversation as the hall slowly filled to capacity.

A full orchestra and choir was gradually assembling, and the instrumentalists began to tune up as they prepared to accompany the singing. The brightly lit stage was filling with row upon row of black cassocked dignitaries.

'Blimey,' sighed Rosie, who was in the aisle seat

with Margaret Briggs beside her, 'they look like a bunch of penguins.' She then proceeded to undo her blouse buttons in order to feed the baby. Margaret did her best to shield Rosie's state of undress from the aged clergyman beside her, but it was evident that he had flushed red with embarrassment. He turned his back on Margaret and Rosie, as if in disgust.

Once the baby was settled and Margaret had wrapped the shawl around Rosie to provide some sense of decorum, Rosie began to look along the rows of 'ordinands' in the hope of seeing Geoff.

'There he is... third on the left, second row... he's smiling.' Rosie was very excited. She turned round to Danny who was seated right behind her. 'There he is... can you see him?'

'Yep... right on.' Danny stood up, placed two fingers in his mouth, and gave an ear-piercing whistle. He then waved wildly at the minister who was his friend. Geoff looked across, slightly raised his hand, and surreptitiously returned the greeting.

Geoff leant back in his chair, he should have warned the people from Redbrook about the niceties of Methodist gatherings. 'Psst' came a noise from the row behind him, and he turned to look into the face of Janet Winter. 'How's it goin'?'

Geoff smiled warmly. 'Janet... great to see you! How's Shetland?'

'Brill, Geoff. Best move I ever made, going there. The place is beautiful and the people are great. We're really seeing the Lord move. How's Sarah?'

Geoff flushed with embarrassment. 'She's pregnant!'

'Congrats all round,' Janet whispered. 'And how's your spiritual life?'

'I really don't like to admit this, but I've been baptised in the Holy Spirit.' Geoff grinned.

'Well praise the Lord for that,' she grinned in return, 'I bet you're an even better darts player now.'

'Funny you should say that...' and before he could finish, the full orchestra had launched into the introduction for the first hymn. The service was about to begin.

The whole congregation stood for Charles Wesley's famous ordination hymn, and as Geoff sang he looked out over the huge crowd to where the Redbrook contingent were standing.

Jesus, thy wandering sheep behold!
See, Lord, with tenderest pity see...

Yes, there was Danny, sat next to his dad Adam and the twins. And just in front was Rosie, holding the baby...

The sheep that cannot find the fold,
Till sought and gathered in by thee.

And then he saw Margaret, radiant with joy... and Bert, in an aisle seat with the dog lying quietly beside him.

Thou, only thou, the kind and good
And sheep-redeeming Shepherd art:

And then, just beside Pete, he thought he saw the

robust figure of Stan Menston... singing loudly as usual... with Molly by his side. The folk from Gospel End must have come as well!

Collect thy flock, and give them food
And pastors after thine own heart.

And there was Alan Drifford, senior steward of Gospel End, his hand raised in praise to God, swaying in rhythm with the tune. In front of him were the other lads from the BC gang, standing between Pip and Miriam and looking overawed by it all.

And there, in the front row of the hall, was his Sarah. She was standing beside John and Jenny from Gospel End, who were sharing a hymnsheet and obviously quite engrossed in each other's company.

Sarah gazed up at him with wide eyes as she sang, and as their eyes met it seemed that time stood still... and they shared what seemed like a lifetime of memories. Geoff returned to the words of the hymn, tears falling down his cheeks, and sang with confidence...

Give the pure word of general grace,
And great shall be the preacher's crowd;
Preachers, who all the sinful race
Point to the all-atoning blood.

'Open their mouth, and utterance give;
Give them a trumpet voice, to call
On all the world to turn and live,
Through faith in him, who died for all...